THE ANTIQUE DEALERS

Suzanne Escott

ISBN: 0692849688
ISBN 13: 9780692849682
Library of Congress Control Number: 2017902679
Suzanne Escott, Martins Ferry, OH

Special thanks to Meg Geroch and Dennis Westbrook.

1

It was a cold and dismal winter's day back in the 1950's as John Ryder drove an old but durable Ford pickup across America's first suspension bridge the Wheeling Suspension Bridge. The bridge spans the Ohio River between Wheeling Island and Wheeling, West Virginia. Allen, John's ten-year-old son, sat sullenly while looking out of the window, watching as a large, coal-filled barge set heavy in the cold Ohio River as it headed south. Allen was not feeling well this morning, which was nothing new for him. The bowl of cereal he had for breakfast that morning was not sitting well in his stomach.

Although his father was smoking, the truck's windows remained closed against the cold, adding to the usual stale cigarette stench that identified the truck as belonging to him. His father had showered and shaved that morning, but he still had that smell of alcohol about him from the night before. An alcoholic always had that smell. The stifling truck's heater was blasting away, adding to the queasy feelings in the boy's stomach. He daydreamed of what it would be like to be on that barge headed south.

Trying to keep his mind on something other than his queasy stomach, he was trying not to vomit and irritate his father. Also there was always the stress of not knowing how the day would end. So often, that was when the nightmare began. He quietly opened his window just a crack, hoping his father wouldn't notice and order him to close it again.

As they came off the bridge, the truck made a right turn onto Main Street and headed through downtown Wheeling. They drove past the Capital Music Hall where entertainers who were big names in country music entertained on Saturday nights. People traveled from all over the country and Canada to attend these shows. The marquee showed that Loretta Lynn would be playing there that evening. The traffic moved slowly as they made their way on down through the downtown area and into the southern residential area.

John drove more slowly now, checking out the houses from side to side. In this area, most of the houses were built in the early and middle 1800s. They had a run-down appearance and looked as though they were barely hanging on to life.

"I think this is it right here," said John, more to himself than to his son.

He'd gotten the address from a name that was listed in the obituaries a week ago. He parked the truck on the street in front of the house that looked as if the owners could neither afford to keep it maintained nor maybe just did not care anymore. The boy followed his father as he walked up onto the front porch and knocked on the door.

John took a couple steps back after knocking, the polite thing to do for a stranger knocking on the door. It allowed the person opening the door not to feel quite so threatened. That was one thing about John. He did know how to be polite. An elderly woman wearing a housedress covered with a sweater and an old handmade shawl for warmth opened the door, giving them a hard look through the glass storm door.

John looked pleasant with his smiling face and warm greeting, "Good morning, ma'am." With his brown hair neatly combed, he looked neat and clean standing there in his blue denim jeans and blue jacket. Allen was dressed in the same manner as his father. John gave her a moment to look them over, and then before she had time to speak, he said in a soft and gentle voice, "I wanted to know if you might have some old junk or furniture that you don't need anymore. We would be glad to take it off your hands for you, at no cost to you. We've had some hard times, and I'm just trying to earn a few dollars to take care of my family." He motioned toward his son.

The woman stood with a blank expression on her wrinkled, pale face that was nearly as white as her cottony, snowy hair. She looked at the boy, perhaps remembering her hard times. She paused as if trying to decide if she should let these strangers into her house.

She thought they did have a friendly and clean appearance, so she did try to think if she did have anything that she wanted to get hauled away. "No, I don't have anything that anybody would want," she said in a curt manner that the elderly sometimes used to appear stronger than they were, especially those not used to being approached by strangers.

"We'd be interested in taking a look, if you don't mind," John said, not wanting to give up easily. "Maybe we could even pay you a few dollars, if you have something that we could use?" John spoke in the kindest and most sincere voice that he could muster.

She just stood there looking at them as they tried to look as respectful and polite as they could. *I could use any money they might pay me*, she thought to herself.

"Come on in then." She opened the door for them. "We can go down to the basement from the kitchen." She turned and led the way through the living room to the kitchen.

The heat in the kitchen and the cooked food smells were almost overpowering to Allen. He could hardly breathe. They followed the woman as she opened a door at the far end of the small kitchen, and they all went on down the steep and narrow basement steps. At least the basement was dry, which was one good thing. Cobwebs and things piled everywhere filled it. It looked like many other older basements. Things were stored year after year and then forgotten.

At least, thought Allen, *the air is cold. It helps to alleviate my nausea.*

"I don't think that I see anything here that we'd be much interested in," said John as he walked around the basement, lifting things up here and there, moving some things, and looking underneath others.

Allen obediently waited by the steps, watching his father.

"I didn't think you would," said the woman, disappointed she would not be getting any money from him.

"If you want us to," said John, "the boy and I could clean out some of this stuff here for you. We might find something that we could use, and you wouldn't have all this mess. Would that be all right with you?"

"Well, I just don't know," said the woman.

"What about that old cupboard over there? It's falling apart and everything, but maybe I could fix it up a little. Maybe use it for something. And what about those old tools? You probably won't be needing those anymore, will you?"

"No, I guess not."

"Does that door over there open to the backyard?"

"Yes, it does," she said.

"If it's okay with you, I'll just pull the truck around through the alley, into the back here." John looked around the basement. Then while looking directly at the woman, he said, "Now so that we understand each other, ma'am, I'll take that old cabinet and the tools." He looked around some more. Then he pointed to one area of the basement. "If you let us have those, we'll take all this stuff over here for you, at no cost to you. Is that okay with you?"

"Yes. I guess so." The woman was trying hard to think if she were doing the right thing. "As long as it doesn't cost me anything, I suppose it'd be all right." Then trying to take charge of the situation, she stood a little taller. "I don't know why you want all that old stuff. But go ahead and take it, if you want to."

John told Allen, "Go stand outside the basement door, so when I drive around to the back, I'll know for sure just where to pull in behind the house."

The old woman went back up the stairs, out of the cold, to the comfort of her afghan blanket and TV set. John pulled the truck around and backed up to the basement door. He started with the cupboard first, taking off the doors and then undoing the back, knowing beforehand that the top was moveable from the bottom piece and the backs could be taken off.

In this way, one man and a ten-year-old boy could move an old six-foot-tall cabinet and stack the pieces so it took up little space in the truck. When that was completed, they started on the pile of things they had agreed to haul away for her. It included four pressback chairs and some damaged spindles, but they could fix those. There was also a medium-sized oak plant stand. The varnish was worn through on the top, but since it was oak, it should finish nicely. And there was an old, beat-up bench. One exceptionally old box of toys looked as if they'd been in the box for years. Lastly, they gathered up the tools and put them into the truck. Allen sat and waited in the truck while his father closed and locked the basement door from the inside.

Then John went up the steps. Upon entering the kitchen, he called out, "Hello?"

The old woman came into the kitchen from the living room. As soon as she saw him, John spoke up, "Just wanted to let you know that we're all loaded up and ready to go now, ma'am. I did lock the basement door so you don't have to go back down into that cold basement."

"Thank you. I'm sorry I didn't have anything more useful to you," she said.

"That's okay," said John. "Sometimes it works out; other times it doesn't. Glad I could help you out a little bit by getting rid of some of that stuff for you. We'll be going now, ma'am," he said again, walking toward the front door. "You have a good day now, ma'am."

"Thank you. Good-bye." The woman closed the door behind him.

He climbed into the truck, and as he turned the key, Allen joined him as he gave a familiar little laugh. "We did good today, boy! Yes, sirree! We did good today!"

"Yea. We did good today," Allen repeated his father's words, full of hope that the day would remain a good day.

"You know, if we didn't take this stuff, somebody else would've probably charged her a lot of money to haul it to the dump. Most people are too ignorant to know the value of stuff like this. That's where your daddy's smarter than most people." He sat up tall in his seat.

With their loaded truck, they headed north on Market Street to an antique store located near the Center Market area. After they had parked the van in the alley behind an old antique store, John told Allen to help him get the bench out of the back and put it up front, turning it upside down in the front seat. John wanted to keep it until he could show it to Linda Stanton at her antique store in another town near the Pennsylvania border, a fifteen-minute drive from Wheeling. Linda was the type of dealer who dealt primarily with old primitive, handmade types of antiques. The bench was something that he felt she would be interested in buying from him. If not, he could always bring it back to this dealer.

John told Allen to wait by the truck and keep watch while he went into the store, hoping the owner was not busy with a customer and would be able to come out to the truck and look at what he had to sell.

John soon returned with the storeowner following behind him to the truck. The antique dealer immediately started going through their truckload of junk. After looking through the things for a few minutes, he turned John. "I'll give you twenty-five dollars for that set of matching chairs, ten dollars each for the tables, seventy-five for the cabinet, twenty-five for the tools, and thirty-five for the toys."

John knew this was a fair amount and nodded a yes because the antique dealer would have to do the repairs. Once the repairs were completed, he would then be able to sell these things for four times what he had paid for them. That was all right with John, and he followed the storeowner back into the store so the dealer could pay him in cash. John had a regular job at the local steel mill, so this was extra money for the alcohol that he and his wife consumed.

John and Allen unloaded the items and put them into the storage area in the back part of the building. John was an expert at knowing what every antique dealer in the area was interested in carrying in his or her store. There were times that he found things that would not fit into his pickup. In those instances, he gave the information to the dealer. If they bought what he had told them about, they paid him a finder's fee. Either way, it was a right sideline for John. His father always said, "If you have a pickup truck, you always have a job. You'll never starve."

They put the bench in the back of the truck and headed for Linda Stanton's antique store that she had on the first floor of her home. They arrived at her place, an older, large Victorian house with a large front porch that sat on Main Street, just beyond the main downtown area in West Alexander, Pennsylvania. Inside was a cluttered look of old butter churns, pottery items once used to hold milk or home-brewed whiskey, and handmade chairs, tables, and benches. Allen saw old handmade cabinets and trunks. Old-time pictures hung on the walls.

"Get you some coffee?" Linda asked as she walked down from her upstairs after hearing the sound of the bell, letting her know some-one had entered the house.

She was a little above average height, a large-boned woman car-rying more weight than was good for her. Wearing an old-fashioned housedress and her shoulder-length hair that never seemed to be un-der control made her look older than her years.

"No thanks. We're sorta busy today," John replied. "Got a bench out in the truck you might be interested in."

"Let's go have a look." She was interested in the bench but tried not to show it too much. Just like the other dealers, she was very care-ful of how much she paid out for anything.

They finally agreed on thirty-five dollars for the bench. She would probably sell it for $125 without doing anything to it other than a good cleaning.

When John and Allen returned home, May Beth, the beautiful bleach-blonde wife and mother, was still in her robe, sitting comfort-ably in front of the TV set with her cigarette in one hand and her beer in the other, watching a movie. She had already gotten a good start on the evening drinking.

Allen helped himself to a glass of milk while his dad got himself a beer from the refrigerator. Both sat down at the kitchen table. After a few moments, John walked into the living room. May Beth ignored him and continued watching her television program.

"How about fixing us something to eat?" John asked in a gruff voice.

May Beth, not happy about having to leave her movie, got up and dragged herself into the kitchen with the cigarette still in her hand. "What'll you want?" she asked, not overjoyed at the thought of having to cook supper.

John went up to her for a playful hug, but she shrugged him off and stepped away from him. "There's ground beef in the refrigerator," said John in a passive voice. "How about some fried potatoes and hamburger patties?"

"Yeah. I guess so," said May Beth, still not enthused about the idea of cooking. She reached for the potatoes. The cigarette was now hanging out of the side of her mouth. "You could've picked something up for dinner while you were downtown. I work too, you know." She started to peel the potatoes. "This is my day off. I need my rest. So how much did you do today?"

"Not much, only about thirty-five dollars." John was not about to tell her the truth of how much he had made off that old furniture.

He knew that she would just think of ways to spend it on her, and she didn't do anything to earn any of it. Also he knew that later, although she had a full-time job at the clothing factory, he would have to buy her beers at the bar. Although she was beautiful and he felt lucky to have her, sadly he knew that she did not feel the same for him.

After she had put the food on the table, May Beth took her dinner to the living room to eat while she watched the rest of her movie. Allen was still eating when John finished and sat there, waiting for his coffee to cool enough to drink. He watched his son eat and wondered to himself just who in their family he looks like. He's heard rumors. They just better not be true. "You did a good job today. I like the way you keep your mouth shut and do as you're told. The one thing I want you never to forget is that other people are just stepping-stones for you to get what you want in life, no matter what it is. A man has to look out for himself."

"Yeah, I know, Pa." His father had told him that same thing so often that the words were now imprinted in his mind.

Later that evening, John and May Beth left Allen at home alone while they went to the Hill Bar. Both were very popular there and greeted warmly when they walked in the door. They joined some friends at their table and ordered a beer. Soon people were calling for John to play the piano. Graciously he carried his beer with him as he went to the piano and started playing an old, familiar tune, "Blues in the Night." Then he went into playing "Blue Skies." A few people started singing with him. A song-and-dance man at heart, John would entertain the people at the bar for hours.

May Beth, always one for a good time, joked and laughed with the others at their table, all the while trading glances with another man seated at the bar. It was late in the evening as people were starting to leave that John sang and played "I'll Be Seeing You." Several times John noticed May Beth going up to the bar to get her beer, rubbing her body against Richard Johnson sitting at the bar and then laughing and talking with him.

John tried to ignore the rumor around town that Allen was Richard Johnson's son. But seeing the way May Beth acted when she was around him made his blood boil.

In the early morning hours, the door to the boy's bedroom was flung open and hit against the wall with a loud bang. Instinctively the boy quickly rose and was about to jump out of bed when his father roughly grabbed him by his shoulder and flung him across the room.

As he bounced from the wall, his father grabbed him again and threw him down on the floor, screaming at him, kicking, and punching him as best as he could in his drunken condition.

The boy did not hear or understand a word that his father was yelling at him. He never heard the words that his father screamed at him during these beatings. He just curled himself into a fetal position for protection, retreating into himself, trying to block out the hurt and the pain, and wondering why his father would beat him like this. He thought they had a good day. His dad had said they had a good day. Why?

2

Twenty years later, several of the steel mills in the area had closed, leaving the workers having to find new careers. This had also been a traumatic experience for the white-collar workers and other managers who were used to a much better lifestyle than the average worker did. Most were in their fifties and sixties years of age and were finding it difficult to find new employment or career at their age. Many were selling their beautiful furniture and moving out of the area.

In a feverish pitch, the bid went up to six thousand dollars before four of the five remaining bidders, one by one, dropped out of the bid. The auctioneer slammed the gavel down with the word "Sold!" The audience applauded the sale of the handsome and elegant Victorian bedroom set that was made of fine mahogany wood.

The winner of the bid, a man in his early sixties, was of medium size with a distinguished-looking, full head of thick, white hair. Pleasantly, the man accepted congratulations from those seated near him as he gathered his coat and proudly headed for the cashier's table. After paying the cashier and receiving a receipt marked "paid in full," he headed for the parking lot to get the pickup that he'd borrowed from his son.

He walked with a spring in his step as he imagined the look on his granddaughter's face when she'd see what he had bought for her. He pulled the truck up to the loading area, wishing that his son hadn't had to work that day and could've accompanied him to the auction. However, he would come by after work to pick up his truck and help his father unload the bedroom set and store it in the half of the garage that was his wife, now deceased, would no longer use.

The old man smiled to himself, knowing that his son would be pleased with the purchase, even though he'd scold his father for spending so much money for a wedding present. After all, five other grandchildren would be expecting this same generosity when they married.

A man associated with the auction checked the old man's paid receipt and then started to help him load the furniture into the pickup. Two other men quietly pitched in to help load up the furniture, as others had assisted them in the past. Another man wearing a blue baseball cap who was standing near them saw them struggling with the chest of drawers and began helping them as the man with the auction withdrew to his post to help another customer. The old man had climbed up into the back of the truck to guide each piece into place and place protective blankets so nothing would get scratched in transit.

"This is a beautiful set that you've got here. I was looking at this myself," said the man in the blue ball cap as he looked up at the old man.

The other men also made comments of appreciation of the fine quality of the furniture.

"Thank you. I saw it advertised in the promotion flyer last week and decided this might make a nice wedding gift for my granddaughter. Then when I saw it, I knew, no matter what it cost, I was getting it for her. Of course, I hoped it wouldn't go up as high as it did, but I guess it's worth it."

"I think you got a good deal," said the man in the blue cap.

The other men helping to load the truck agreed with him as they helped to slide the five-foot-tall chest in place against the side of the truck. The men took the mirror off the dresser, covered the top with a blanket, and set it on its side next to the chest. The dresser mirror was covered with a blanket and then placed between the dresser and the chest. The headboard and footboard were wrapped in blankets and placed beside the dresser.

"Thank you, all of you, for your help," the old man said as he got down from the loaded truck. Then he reached into the front of the truck for the rope he'd brought with him.

"We'll just make sure that this is tied down good. Then you can be on your way," said the man in the blue ball cap as he took one end of the rope that the man had already thrown over the load.

As the men helped him tie down the load, the old man said, "I can't wait to see my granddaughter's face when I give her this. She's going to love it."

The men nodded and commented with words, agreeing with the old man as he continued talking while they finished tying up the load.

"Lord knows that jerk she's marrying will never get her anything like this, but you can't tell the young anything that they don't want to hear. She's madly in love and blind to anything else." Then he smiled at them. "No doubt I was the same way when I was her age."

"Yeah. That's just the way life is," said the man wearing the blue ball cap as he finished the last tie down and then stepped back. "Do you have someone to help you unload when you get home?"

"Yes. My son will come and help me when he gets off work. Thanks again for your help."

The other men who'd been helping waved an arm in a "you're welcome; it's nothing" way as they went back to the auction area.

"You're welcome," said the man in the blue ball cap as he slowly backed away from the truck as it started pulling away.

He tried not to draw attention to himself as he walked quickly to his van parked nearby. He'd made a point of arriving early to the auction, just for that purpose of being able to park where he could make a quick getaway.

He let the man and his truck get a little way ahead of him before he followed the truck out onto the highway, staying just far enough behind to keep the truck in sight. They took the entrance ramp and headed south on Interstate 79. He continued following as the truck exited the interstate and drove on a two-lane road that entered a small town.

The truck turned down a side street with well-groomed older homes with shade trees and bushes on either side of the street and long driveways. As the truck slowed down to turn up a driveway, he slowed his van and watched as the man's garage door opened by remote. He casually backed his van up the driveway and parked back-to-back to the man's truck, now parked inside the garage.

"Hey there!" he said to the bewildered-looking old man as he jumped out of his van and walked up to him with a big, friendly grin on his face. "I was worried about you and that heavy furniture. So when I saw that I was coming this same way, I thought to myself that it wouldn't hurt me none to give you a hand."

"Why thank you. Do you live around here?"

"No. I was just on my way to visit a friend who lives on up the highway. When I saw you turn in here, I thought I'd just take a few moments and help you out, if I could." He noticed that no one else appeared to be at home in the house.

"Well," the old man said, still a little confused, "that's nice of you to go out of your way like this. I was going to call my son when he gets home from work to come over and help me, but if you don't mind, I think the two of us can handle it. I'll be storing it here until my granddaughter gets moved into her new home in a couple months."

"No problem. I can help you do that."

They had untied the load and were taking off the blankets for the chairs when the old man felt just a brief moment of pain. As he fell to his knees, he turned with a bewildered look on his face and looked up at his killer. After another quick blow to the head, the beautiful white head of hair was now crimson red as the man lay dead on the garage floor.

The killer's adrenaline was pumping as he quickly slid the furniture from the back of the pickup and got into the back of his van.

After covering the furniture with the blankets, he put the rope with his fingerprints into the van. *Chances are,* he thought, *no one around here will even know that the old man had even bought any furniture.* So he took the man's wallet to leave the impression that the man was killed for his money.

After wiping any possible fingerprints from the back of the man's truck, he used a piece of rag to press the garage-door button to close the door, leaving the man lying in a pool of his own blood next to his truck. He threw the rag into the back of the van as he closed the back doors of his van and got in the drivers' seat.

He took a deep breath and let it out slowly. Then he casually drove down the driveway and made a right turn to get back to the highway.

He arrived at the storage unit that he rented a few weeks ago and unloaded his newly acquired Victorian bedroom set. He'd soon have enough furniture to fill a large rental truck to make a long haul Down South or maybe to California. People there had lots of money to spend on nice furniture. Of course, he'd tell everyone that he was going somewhere else.

Later that evening, Michael Johnson, twenty-eight-year-old son of Richard and Sara Johnson, owners of Johnson's Antique and Refinishing Store, arrived at his parents' home for dinner. He was a tall and slender man with a full head of hair and a well-trimmed beard. Their property was once a small farm with twenty-five acres. In their driveway, he saw a white van with a Texas license plate that he wasn't familiar with seeing. They rarely had visitors.

He entered through the kitchen door. Stirring something on the stove, his mother was a small, gray-haired woman whose legs and arms were so thin that she reminded people of a delicate bird.

"Whose van?" asked Michael as he looked in the living room and saw only his father Richard dozing, seated in his recliner with his oxygen tank on the floor beside him.

Many years of smoking had brought the once strong and hand-some man who had the problem of women throwing themselves at him in his younger years to this now emaciated-looking man suffering with emphysema. He had hired Franny Woodling to manage the store for them, much to the chagrin of his son Michael, now recovering from drug and alcohol problems. Franny is dependable and honest, however a little too competent and efficient for Michael's way of thinking. The two have their moments of disagreements.

"Allen's here from Texas! We were so surprised when he called this morning saying that he might be here for a while. He's not sure for how long. Says he wants to see how we do things at the store.

"So where is he?" Michael asked.

"He's resting upstairs in his old room. That was a long drive from Texas. It took him two days. He was going to stay at his parents' old house, but your father told him to come here and stay. That place hasn't been touched in years. Wake up your father, and let's eat."

While they were having coffee after dinner, Michael said, "I'd like for you to see this Chippendale chest that I bought today. I've got it out in the van." He usually didn't like to show it when he was proud of himself, but with this, he couldn't help but let his elation show.

"A real Chippendale?" his father asked. "Where did you get it?"

As they walked out to the van, his father dragging his oxygen tank behind him, Michael told him how he acquired the chest, "I was at a flea market in Wintersville, and this guy told me that he has this Chippendale chest that he'd like to sell right away. He needed the money. I followed him home. He has a beautiful home filled with quality antique furnishings. He said his son is in trouble in Las Vegas and needs money. He wanted thirty-five hundred dollars, so I gave it to him. He's one of those who lost his job when the steel mill shut down."

"It's sad how life has changed for so many," said Sara.

"Yes, it is. But Michael got a bargain", said Richard. This is worth at least ten thousand dollars." Richard pulled out the bottom drawer and turned it over to see how the bottom of the drawer was made.

"No nails or screws here." You'd better take this to the store for safe-keeping until you can find a buyer," Richard said as he replaced the drawer.

"Good idea," said Michael. "There's a guy in Cadiz who I think might be interested in this. He loves this stuff, and he has the money."

"Get Allen to go with you to unload this so it doesn't get scratched."

Several years ago, Richard told Allen and then Michael and his younger brother Richard Jr. that he was Allen's real father. He felt guilty that he allowed Allen to grow up with a man who would often beat and ridicule him. So he took Allen into their home after John Ryder murdered his mother, May Beth. It was amazing how much alike Michael and Allen were and how well they got along with each other.

"Franny changed the locks on the doors at the store, so you'll have to go by her place and get a key. She always keeps an extra copy of keys hanging by her back door," said Sara.

"I'll go and get Allen and take care of this right now." Michael then went to the guest room.

When he opened the door, Allen opened his eyes and grinned. "Hey, Michael, hope you don't mind my coming here. Got homesick and wanted to drive some roads that I know. That was my favorite thing to do here. My wife left me." He shrugged his shoulders. "Since I served my time in the air force, I've been having a rough time support-ing my family, so she took the kids and went back with her parents."

"You're not alone. My wife and kids are now staying with her par-ents. Said I drank too much, among other things. I haven't had a drink for three months, so I hope I'm over the hard part. I'm staying in the mobile home up on the far side of the property again." Michael paused. "I need you to help me unload a chest out at the store."

"Sure thing," said Allen.

"Dinner is on the stove, so we will eat something before we go."

"I'll be downstairs in a few minutes." Allen gulped down some of the leftover dinner before joining Michael in his van, and they rode to Franny's house.

Allen waited in the car for him while Michael ran up the steps to Franny's house to get a key. He could hear Franny call after Michael, "Don't forget to bring that key back tonight."

"You've got another one!" Michael called back.

"And I always want an extra key."

"Okay. I'll bring it back."

They arrived at the store. "Wow!" exclaimed Allen. "You've turned this into quite a store. A lot different from when I was last here."

"I hate to admit it, but this is all Franny's doing. She has quite a touch for this sort of thing." After unloading the chest, Michael said, "Well, let's drop off Franny's key and head back home. It's been a long day, probably for you too with all that driving."

"A good night's rest would be great," replied Allen.

3

The next day was a Sunday. Michael took Allen with him to spend the day with him at a large outdoor flea market with over four hundred vendors.

"You never know what you might find at one of these places," said Michael.

They strolled up one aisle and down another, stopping to look more carefully at one thing or another. They got junk food from the outdoor concession stands. They both enjoyed forgetting about their cares and worries for the day. They also talked about Michael's home inspection and appraisal business that he worked from home, in addition to the antique business.

"I sure wish that I'd thought about something like that to earn a living. Houston would be a great place to be an appraiser."

"I'll teach you what I know, and I have a few books that tell you how to do a good job."

"That would be great. Thank you, Michael."

Michael bought a couple of small items he thought his kids might like to have before they headed home.

The next morning, a beautifully restored, white 1968 Ford Mustang came down Main Street in Wheeling and pulled into its usual parking space behind Johnson's Antiques and Refinishing Store. Franny had arrived for work.

She was an average-looking person of medium height and weight with brown hair and eyes. However, even dressed in denim, she exuded an air of grace and elegance as she quickly walked to the back door, unlocked it, and went inside the store.

A few minutes later, a blue pickup turned in and parked next to the car. Davy Randolph was wearing his usual T-shirt and jeans. He was a tall, handsome young man in his middle thirties with neat, brown, curly hair. Davy did most of the paint and varnish stripping and the refinishing work for the store. Usually two local high-school boys came in after school a couple afternoons a week and sometimes on Saturdays to help Davy with the work.

The store was located on lower Market Street, catty-corner to the Center Market, the home of Coleman's Fish Market. At lunchtime, customers formed a long line as they waited to place their takeout order for white fish sandwiches with chips and soft drinks.

In addition to fish, there were vendors within the block-long building who catered to the tourist trade, selling items made in West Virginia, things of the Appalachian culture. On either side of Coleman's were several antique stores, a coffee shop, a couple of quaint restaurants, a store that sold old books, an artist's studio, a dance studio, and several buildings that had apartments above their commercial venues. The area was known as a unique tourist area of Wheeling.

Inside Johnson's, Franny had walked through to the front of the building and unlocked the front door, placing a few country-style items—an old spinning wheel and two handmade kitchen chairs—outside in front of the store for decoration. Then she returned to the back of the building, joining Davy with a cup of coffee as they proceeded with their usual routine of going over the furniture items that needed to be worked on that day.

Parked inside the back loading dock doors sat the company van. On this morning, sitting in front of the van, out of view of any prying eyes from the windows, sat a beautiful chest that wasn't there when they'd left on Saturday. The two front legs of the chest had the ball and claw-foot of an original Chippendale.

Both walked over for a closer inspection. The chest was about five feet tall and three feet wide with five drawers. After just a quick look, Franny could see that this was indeed an extraordinarily fine piece of furniture with a dignity and personality of its own.

It was easy to see that the mahogany wood had been well cared for with its original finish and was truly aged wood, not some re-production that was so common today. She pulled out one of the drawers and turned it over to see if the bottom of the drawer were beveled. It was, and the dovetails holding the drawer together were handmade.

Looking into the space where the drawer went, she looked at the age of the wood on the inside, just to make sure the wood inside was indeed aged. It was. Dust covers were between each drawer. The back of the chest was made with real wood instead of some prefabri-cated type of wood that had been used during the past seventy years. The chest was put together with wood dowels instead of metal wood screws. Mahogany from the Caribbean was the top choice of wood for fine furniture in the 1700s and early 1800s, when this chest was probably made. It was truly a beautiful antique.

"My God. This is awesome," said Franny with admiration as she looked more closely at the chest. "A good cleaning up, but otherwise, this is in excellent condition."

"Yeah. Michael must have brought this in over the weekend," said Davy. "He can sure find some good ones, can't he?"

Michael was the only tenant who had a key to the store since his father was the owner. So it was not unusual for them to come into work and find a piece that wasn't there when they'd left for the day.

"He sure can," said Franny.

Franny heard the sound of the bell that rang whenever someone entered the front of the store. She quickly walked to the front of the store where they had antiques for sale. Quite often, people would bring things for refinishing in the front door. Larger items were unloaded in the back. Franny got her exercise going from one end of the store to the other, waiting on customers.

Upon entering the front area, she saw a young woman who had brought in four country kitchen chairs. Two were heavily painted white; the other two had been painted black. She could see where the woman had tried to strip one of them herself and gave up on the idea. All of them were filthy, as if they'd spent the last several years in the corner of a barn somewhere, which was probably where they'd been. It seldom happened that customers cleaned something before bringing it into Johnson's. That was the main reason that Franny and her assistant at the store, Belle Walker, dressed in a casual way, wearing the type of clothes they didn't have to worry about getting dirty.

"Hello," said Franny in one her most pleasant manners.

"Hi," said the woman. "I have these chairs that I'd like to have stripped. There's also a wooden kitchen table that's still in my truck. I can varnish them myself, but I was wondering how much you think it'd cost just to have them stripped."

"Well, let me go take a look at the table, and I can give you a price."

They both walked out to the girl's pickup parked in front of the store.

Franny quickly assessed the quality and condition of the table. "This is a nice set that you have. Let's see. That would be forty-five for each chair and eighty-five for the table. But," she said as she looked underneath the table, "I'd like to warn you about taking off this old paint. Quite often, someone has painted over the bare wood. Then the paint soaks down into the grain. So now, when you try to strip them, you can't get all of the paint out, and it keeps working its way to the surface. You may end up having to paint them again."

"Well," the woman said as she pondered over that information for a moment, "I think that I'd like to go ahead and have you strip them. At least get some of the layers off."

Franny helped her carry the table into the store and made out a receipt for the furniture. "I'll call you when they're ready." She handed her a copy of the receipt.

"Thank you," said the young woman as she walked out the door.

Franny placed the table along with the chairs in the room behind the showroom area. At the sound of the doorbell, she looked up to see Jerry Manning, one of the store's tenants, entering the store. Jerry, a handsome man in his early fifties, had his black hair showing just a bit of gray at his temples. He was still looking good in blue jeans after several years of handling antique furniture.

Even with people he'd known for a long time, he couldn't hide the nervousness that he'd had since his hard and traumatic childhood. He started off each meeting with an outgoing and exuberant greeting, hoping that one wouldn't notice his stuttering. He got himself under control after a few moments and then spoke without the stuttering, only to have it appear again when excited. And he was easily excited.

"H-h-h-hey, s-s-s-sailor girl," he said, his way of degrading her. Deep down, he believed, along with several other men on this planet that women shouldn't be in charge of anything outside of the home. Also all women needed to be under the control of a man, and if one were not, it was his choice whether they should be under his control. "W-w-w-w-what's g-going on in here?" And he immediately started nosing around the room to see what furniture had come and gone since he'd last been there.

With an uninspired "hi," Franny entered a workroom just beyond the showroom and began preparations to put a final coat of finish on a beautiful walnut table before customers started coming in. This type of table was one that people would normally use to place a lamp or some other decorative object on.

Being ignored, Jerry gave a sound of "humph" and wandered into the back to see what Davy was doing. Jerry rented a space there to sell his antiques and usually came in three or four times a week, naturally hoping that something of his was sold.

He lived alone now that his wife had passed away, and his son, who could not stand any more abuse from him, refused to have anything to do with him. Now the rumor was that a woman and her kids, who had been living with him for the past few months, had left him. Normally people would have sympathy for someone in his position; however, his abrasive personality prohibited people from caring about his well-being.

Jerry usually did his own furniture stripping and refinishing, working in the basement of his home. However recently, he had brought in some things for stripping only. He was always in blue jeans, ball cap, and a jean jacket when the weather wasn't too cold. As an old family friend of Richard Johnson, Jerry had been allowed to wander around the workshop area whenever he pleased. Jerry enjoyed nosing around the store and checking out what had been brought in for refinishing. Quite often he'd see things that had been in auctions within the past few weeks.

He was especially interested in seeing what Michael had bought over the weekend from auctions throughout the tristate area. Quite often, while at an auction, he suspected that someone was actually bidding for Michael. Since dealers could not attend all of the auctions, they'd pay someone else to buy for them. Sometimes these people would buy things at auction that they knew other dealers would be interested in buying from them.

Jerry resented Michael with his arrogant attitude and, of course, because Michael could afford to outbid most of the other dealers in the area. Michael, as well as several of the other dealers in the area, would collect a truckload of antiques and old furniture and haul it to other parts of the country to sell at large auction houses. Michael usually went to the Atlanta auction, where people came from all over the country to buy antiques. That was where Michael made his money.

The one pleasure the other dealers did get sometimes was to bid up the price on Michael and then laugh among themselves when he ended up paying more for an item than he'd wanted to pay. That was why he'd sometimes have someone else bid for him. But it still didn't solve the problem for the other local dealers. They'd have to travel to more sales to keep up their inventory for their stores.

Although Franny wasn't an expert on antique furniture, she managed the store and all of the refinishing work. It was a new career for her after spending the previous twenty years serving with the navy. She was now retired and living back in her hometown on the Ohio side of the Ohio River. Moving here was a cultural shock to her after living in large cities for so many years. Also without her uniform with its stripes denoting her rank, she no longer received the immediate respect that was so much a part of her life.

Her memories of other times and faraway places helped her to appreciate her life, then and now. There was no way to describe the years of beautiful morning sunrises and evening sunsets with the waves of the ocean in the shimmering light. But that was the past. She felt fortunate to have found a job she enjoyed most of the time in her hometown where her soul belonged.

She loved waiting on the customers and working with the furniture. She'd start with a dirty, old piece of furniture and complete the work that went into changing it into a beautiful heirloom for its owner. She loved to see the look on the customer's face when he or she came to pick up his or her cherished antique.

However, as everyone all knew, working with some of those chaotic customers could become a nerve-wracking experience. Sometimes, when all the old paint is taken off, the reason is found why someone decided to paint it in the first place. It could be to cover a horrible stain or burn mark that had marred the piece, or perhaps it had damage due to exposure to the weather. Or in some cases, an animal had chewed into the wood. Sometimes that paint served a purpose, and when it was taken off and some damage was discovered that the customer didn't expect, he or she was not happy and took it out on Franny. Sometimes the customer thought that someone at the store caused the damage. Fortunately those instances were rare. Luckily most of the customers were good, sensible people.

The first half of the store was the showroom area, filled with beautiful antiques. Dealers, who couldn't afford it or didn't want to be bothered with the hassle of running their own store, paid Johnson's for rental space to show and sell some of their antiques. Most of the antiques were furniture. However, one dealer, Marge Fodor, specialized in glassware made in the Imperial Glass and Fostoria Glass factories that once flourished in the local area. Her father had worked as a glass blower at the Imperial Glass Factory across the river in Bellaire, Ohio. The large glass factories had all been shut down for several years now due to imports and the use of plastics.

Marge had four showcases filled with the expensive glassware. These cases were kept locked, except when a customer requested to get a better look. Then Franny or her assistant, Belle, would stay right there with them until the piece was either sold or placed securely back into the case.

Franny had a desk near the back part of the showroom area so she could help wait on customers. Belle, who was home with her grandmother for a few days due to her grandmother's illness, usually manned the checkout counter by the front door. The two had formed their own little side business and paid rent for space so they could sell lace doilies and quilts, mostly made in West Virginia, and old pictures and mirror frames. Franny had become a real expert in the restoring of the old picture and mirror frames. Several were displayed on the walls, many with old prints that she bought from Kirk's Photo Supply Store that was up the street from Johnson's. These pictures and mirrors were affordable and sold quite well as gifts. She usually got her frames from Ray Rouse, another one of the tenants in the store. These type of things were much easier for those arriving there on the tour buses to purchase and take with them.

Franny's and Belle's little business didn't include any items that would be in competition with the other dealers in the store. They were paid minimum wage for managing the day-to-day activities of the store, along with a sales commission on all of the sales they made for the other space renters. Also they received a small percentage of the stripping and refinishing revenue of the store. This system encouraged them to work as hard as they could to increase business for the store.

Walking in through the front door, people found themselves in a beautiful showroom tastefully filled with the various styles and periods of antique and old furniture. The walls were decorated with Belle's and Franny's beautiful pictures and mirrors, all handmade in West Virginia. Appalachian quilts and doilies were displayed throughout for effect. The pleasant aroma of orange oil they used to polish the furniture filled the air.

The back wall of the showroom area was a two-way mirror. Behind the mirror was a workroom, allowing them a view of the front door and the showroom while they worked on projects rather than sitting around and waiting for customers. Swinging doors on either side of the room took them from the showroom to the work area and on into the back. Beyond this area were double doors with glass windows that opened into the large loading dock area. On the right side of the loading dock area was a large freight elevator used to take furniture to the basement, where there was a flow-over system for fine pieces of furniture, especially soft wood pieces. Also a large, twelve-foot-long by six-feet-wide and three-feet-deep tank filled with stripping chemicals was usually used for heavily painted hardwoods.

A separate room was used to properly dry items that had been stripped. Then they were washed down with a power hose that cleaned off the stripper material and other debris. Off to the side was a clean room, used for spraying a new finish on furniture. An expensive ventilation and exhaust system for both floors, approved by the EPA, prevented the harmful vapors from stripping chemicals from ruining anyone's fish sandwich at the fish market.

Franny placed the table she'd just finished into a separate finishing room to allow the finish to set up free of any dirt that might be in the air. With that done, she began working on what was called a bookcase secretary from the late 1800s. She had already applied two coats of finish from the previous day. So now, she lightly sanded with a sheet of fine sandpaper. Then she'd wash it down with mineral spirits. After waiting for fifteen minutes for it to dry, she'd use a tack cloth to completely remove any debris that might still be on the surface and then apply the last coat of finish. The beauty that each brush stroke brought was like magic taking place right in front of one's eyes.

The secretary had a bookcase area with a glass door, which was about five feet high. To the right of the bookcase was a pull-down lid that formed a desk area. At the back part of which, there were cubbyholes and spaces for storing bills or letters, even a hidden drawer area. Beneath the table were three drawers for miscellaneous items. There was a top to the secretary, above the pull-down lid. Above the top was space for a small mirror that she had taken off and put aside until after the refinishing was completed. She loved the feel of the wood as it became smoother with each sanding. *The customer is going to love this when it's finished,* she thought to herself.

Golden oak was such a beautiful hardwood, so even though this piece was old, Franny had done enough of them to know that, when the refinishing was complete, the customer would be pleased because it was going to turn out to be just beautiful!

Jerry was walking in from the back area, speaking his usual commentary in a fast, nervous, stuttering kind of way. "J-j-j-junk! T-t-t-this s-s-s-s-stuff's all j-j-j-junk!" He waved his arms to signify all the furniture that was in that area. That was his usual comment for anything that wasn't his.

Franny just rolled her eyes and tried to ignore him.

"Who, uh? Who brought in that chest back there? Is that Michael's? I had one b-better than that a couple months ago. S-s-sold it to a guy in Zanesville. Made a pretty good profit on it too. Is that Michael's?"

When he finally shut up, she told him, "No, it isn't Michael's. It belongs to a customer from the Mt. Pleasant area. The trouble is that they don't have a key to unlock it so that we can work on it. None of the keys I have will open it."

"I-I don't mean that c-c-china chest. I mean that Ch-Chippendale back there."

"Oh, that one. No, it belongs to a customer." She knew that Michael couldn't stand the way Jerry nosed around into his business. She didn't like to lie to anyone, but Michael's business was his own. She knew that Jerry would never buy anything that expensive.

"Ah, I-I got a whole box full of keys. There ain't nothing I can't open," said Jerry. Finally he was getting the hint that she wasn't going to tell him anything about the chest. "I'll bring that box of keys up to you after lunch."

Surprised at the offer, Franny said, "Thank you." Jerry wasn't the type to do anything for anyone. She continued working on the table as Jerry nosed around some more.

"Where's ding-dong?"

"She's not here, and please stop referring to Belle like that," she said in a quiet but firm voice. "Just because that was a cute thing to say when you were a little boy that was a long time ago. It doesn't sound very good coming from an old man!" She could tell by the way that he stiffened his body that the "old man" part got to him.

Well, she thought, *he deserves it.*

"Her grandmother is ill. She has to stay home with her for a few days."

"Aw. T-T-That's too bad. W-W-Well, I-I-I got stuff to do. C-Can't waste time hanging around here all day." And he was out the door.

4

J ust then Michael came into the shop. He was neat and attractive
in his uniform of Dockers and a casual shirt. With him was a
young man who smiled at Franny pleasantly. He didn't say anything, and Michael didn't introduce him. The young man also had
dark brown hair. He had a handsome face with a neat appearance
wearing blue jeans and a blue flannel shirt. Franny was struck with
how much he resembled Michael when he turned his head a certain
way. She had the feeling that he might be a relative since Michael was
usually alone.

Michael was not pleased with seeing Jerry as he left the store.
They had words a couple of years ago. Whatever the argument was
about, neither seemed willing to let go of it, and they danced around
each other in a strained but polite way every time they met.

"What did he want?" Michael growled.

"The usual nosing around and getting on people's nerves."

Michael had worked with his father to set up this store and felt
that he deserved anything that he wanted from it. But once Richard
became too ill to work anymore, he gave the management of the store
to Franny, believing that Michael would drain the place and leave
him and Sara without an income.

Richard knew his son because, at first, that was exactly what
Michael tried to do at every opportunity. Whatever profit the store

could have made went into purchasing materials that Michael used up on the stripping and refinishing of his antiques that he sold at a profit to himself. The store never saw any of that money. It had been a struggle, but Franny had finally gotten that under control. When she placed an order for supplies, she'd place a double order on things he usually used and charged it to him.

Michael and the young man walked into the back of the store. It looked to Franny that he was showing the young man the setup of the operation.

The phone rang again. A customer wanted to be sure that Franny was going to be staying late at Johnson's before loading up her furniture and making the long trip. Franny assured the woman that she'd wait for her until six. Then she went back to working on the oak secretary.

After a while, the bell rang, letting her know that someone had entered the front door. She quickly cleaned her hands. She could see through the two-way mirror that the person who came into the store was Joanna McKenzie, a favorite customer at Johnson's. Joanna had seen the beautiful walnut armoire in the front window and had come in to inspect it further.

Although she was in her middle sixties, Joanna was still beautiful with flawless porcelain skin. She'd always maintained her weight. Women half her age were envious of her size and the fit of her clothes. Quite often, she dressed, as she was today, in a richly elegant manner with the type of clothing that gave a light and flowing effect. She wore her medium brown, color-from-a-bottle hair free-flowing down her back, just like a girl in her early twenties. A shy and delicate person, she chose her words carefully, speaking in a softly cultured voice, exuding an air of tranquility and mystery.

There were rumors that Joanna had obtained her wealth by having spent her life as a high-class call girl in New York with her husband as her pimp. Franny thought that was absurd; however, hints of a scandalous life made Joanna an even more exciting and intriguing character. She'd always told Franny that her husband was retired from a stock brokerage firm in New York. Whatever her past was, that was another lifetime ago. Nowadays Joanna quietly spent her time writing romance novels.

"Hello. I see you're busy as usual," said Joanna as she headed for the armoire.

"Thank God things have picked up a bit lately. It's good to see you, as always. How've you been?"

"Just fine, and you?" Joanna looked over at Franny and then focused back on the armoire, gently feeling the softness of the satin finish on the warm and beautiful walnut wood.

"Great now that the weather is giving us a break for a while," Franny said as she joined Joanna at the armoire. "Pretty nice, huh?"

"I wonder what he'll take for this." She chose to ignore the price sticker on the side of the armoire.

"I can find out for you, if you like. I'm pretty sure Michael's still in the back. I'll go and get him, and you can talk to him about what he wants for it."

Michael had told her what he wanted to sell it for and how much to come down on the price to make a sale. But Joanna was a repeat customer, and Franny thought that he'd probably sell it to her at an even lower price.

She walked into the back to get Michael. He was showing the chest he had brought in over the weekend to the young man who came in with him. One could always tell when Michael had found himself an exceptional piece of furniture. He'd rub his hands over it and study every inch of it. He'd enjoy the feel of the wood and think of whom, among his many contacts, would be the most interested in owning this beautiful antique cabinet.

As she walked on back to where he was with the chest, she called out to him, "Michael, Joanna McKenzie is interested in your walnut armoire that's up front. I told her that she could talk to you about how much you want for it."

"Okay," said Michael as he started on up to the front.

Even though he had more than the average number of faults, Michael always spoke in a soft, quiet voice. To the customers, he was a nonthreatening type of person. He gave the impression of being a very honest and sincere man. He would be kind to the delicate Joanna.

Davy had filled the back part of the loading dock area with furniture that he had finished stripping of its old finish. He'd separated the items to be stripped of finish only. The customers would put the finish on themselves from the things that customers wanted to be finished by Johnson's. Tung oil or antique oil finish were completed in the work area that Franny used. It usually took at least six coats of tung oil to make a piece of furniture truly beautiful.

After looking over the work that Davy had finished, Franny went back up to the front to her desk area to call the customers to come and pick up their furniture. Michael was still talking to Joanna about the armoire. The door opened, and a man came in. He tipped his baseball cap, like a kind of salute that some of the older men did in this area, and said, "Hello."

He wanted to buy some antique hardware for a cabinet. Franny got out the hardware catalogs so he could pick out the kind he wanted. She pointed out the ones she carried in stock, and he chose some of those. After paying for them, he looked around the store a while before leaving.

Just then, the phone rang. It always seemed to work this way. There were times when the store was empty and the phone was quiet. Then customers filled the store, and the phone rang constantly. It never failed.

Joanna and Michael settled on a price for the armoire. Also Davy and Michael would deliver the piece to Joanna's house later that evening. Of course, Davy was being volunteered without his knowledge. Joanna left to make sure she had a place to put the armoire when it arrived.

Michael went to the back work area, and a few minutes later, he came back to the front of the store with his friend trailing behind him and headed to the front door.

"You're not going to introduce me to your friend?" asked Franny.

"This is Allen Ryder. He grew up around here until he left for the air force. He was a year behind me in school." Just then Michael's cell phone rang. He went to the far end of the room to answer it.

"Hi. My name is Franny. I'm retired navy."

He seemed surprised. "Twenty years?"

"Twenty years, and I wouldn't mind going back for another twenty. I loved it. Smartest thing I ever did in my life was to join and stay for the twenty years."

"I served four years, mostly in Texas. My family's still there. Four years was enough for me. Don't care for someone telling me what to do all the time."

"I don't know about the air force, but the navy is primarily a mutual respect kind of thing. Everybody knows his or her job and tries to do his or her best at it."

"So that's your Mustang out back," he asked, changing the subject. Apparently Michael had already told him that it was.

"Yes. A friend of mine spent about five years restoring it and then got cancer. Suffered from that for a year before passing away. He left it to me in his will. It still drives great on the highway. I love it."

"Let's go." Michael was finished with his call and tired of standing there, listening to their gab.

Allen waved good-bye as they left the store. All was quiet again for Franny to work on the secretary.

Later that afternoon, Jerry returned with a cigar box full of keys. Franny opened the box and saw every key imaginable. She also had a box of old keys, just in case they might be useful. However, she had to admit that Jerry's box was filled with a great deal more keys than what she had in her box.

Jerry, with a pleased look on his face, said, "I-I-I told you. I-I-I have a key that can open that china cabinet. I can open anything." He was quite proud of himself.

"I hope you're right. Let's go and see if we can open that cabinet," said Franny as she headed for the back where the chest was standing.

"I-I gotta go right now. I-I know you'll be able to open it. I'll pick up those keys tomorrow," called Jerry as he headed toward the front door. "Hey, Franny, are you going to that Barnhart auction down in Sistersville? That'd be a week from this Saturday. That's supposed to be a good one."

"Probably," Franny called back to him as he left through the front door.

She heard the bell that rang whenever someone drove up to the back loading dock. She could see through the windows in the double doors leading from the work area that a large van loaded with several pieces of heavily painted furniture was backing into the loading dock area.

"Hey there, Elroy. How're you doing?" Franny called out to the tall, lanky young man dressed in an old jean jacket and old blue jeans. She walked out to his truck with a customer receipt to greet him and look over the furniture.

"Just fine," said Elroy. "What'd you think it might cost to have this stuff stripped?"

She saw a Hoosier cabinet that was heavily painted white, plus a set of four oak chairs with a matching, large, round, oak, claw-foot table that had a varnish finish. "Usually what we've been doing with the Hoosiers is to take the back off the cabinet and just throw it away because we'd never be able to get the paint out of that plywood backing. We've been using Luan plywood to finish them. It holds a stain really good. They usually turn out really nice that way."

"Yea," said Elroy. "I think you're right about that just being plywood on the back. I've used that Luan plywood before. It does turn out pretty nice. I guess that's what I'll do with this, so go ahead and take off that back and throw it away. That'd be fine."

She gave him a price for stripping the paint off all the pieces in the van. He agreed with the prices, so Davy helped him to unload the van while Franny filled out the work request, listing each item and the cost of stripping the paint off each one.

"I'll need your telephone number," said Franny.

He called out the number to her as she wrote it on the receipt, and then she handed him a copy.

"I'll be calling you, probably sometime next week. Take it easy," Franny said.

"See ya, Franny. Thanks for helping me unload, Davy." Elroy got into his van and drove off.

A little later that afternoon, a man was sitting in his van with a view of the back parking lot of Johnson's. He watched as two young girls passed by him, walking home from high school, stooped under the weight of their backpacks. Shades of pink and orange streaked their long blonde hair. They were wearing black lipstick and matching nails with black tops and blue jeans that looked molded to their bodies. *Kids these days*, he thought to himself. All was quiet in the parking lot.

He watched the people, many of them out-of-town tourists coming and going from the various shops as he listened to the radio. After the time and weather, the newsman stated facts about a man found murdered in his home with no obvious motive for the crime. He smiled to himself and was pleased that he was able to fool so many people.

After another busload of tourists were emptied onto the street, many of them headed toward Johnson's. He started up his van, drove into the back parking lot, and parked near the white Mustang. He nonchalantly got out of his van, walked up to the car, and quickly used a metal bar to unlock the door. He reached in and got the garage-door remote that was attached to the overhead visor and walked back to his van.

Carefully he opened the remote and wrote down the combination. Then he replaced the remote on her car visor and drove to the local Sears store, where he bought the same type of remote and adjusted the setting to match the one from her car. Satisfied and pleased with himself, he set his Garmin to an address he found online and headed for that location.

The workers in Johnson's were busy the rest of the afternoon with people delivering furniture to be worked on and those picking up furniture that had been left there the previous week or two. Customers were also browsing the antique stores in the Center Market area.

Franny had forgotten what an asset it had been to have Belle there, helping with the customers. She enjoyed talking to them about the items they were looking at but almost never buy. They all seemed to have memories or stories about their grandmother having this or that in her home when they were younger. However, when one has other work to get done, sightseers could consume too much of one's time.

It was near closing time when Ray Rouse, another tenant, came in the front door of the store. "Hey, Franny. How're you doing?"

"Well, as Davy would say, finer than a frog's hair," replied Franny as she admired the fine-looking specimen of a man who was walking toward her, his colorful past now lightly engraved on his face.

Ray was tall and well-built, a strikingly handsome man with brown eyes and brown hair that was beginning to gray on the sides, adding to his impressive features. Today he was dressed neatly in a pair of light-colored pants and a medium brown plaid shirt with polished, dark brown boots. One could tell by the way he walked that he felt good about himself and the way he fit into his clothes.

"Oh, those Southern boys, they do have their own colorful language, don't they?"

"Davy does. That's for sure. What's going on with you today?"

"Working on getting things ready for a trip to Texas the week after next. I'm waiting until after that Barnhart estate sale. That's one sale I don't want to miss. Should be quite a sale."

"That's what I've heard. Millie Sanders brought me a flyer to put in the window." She pointed to the poster in the front window.

"That Barnhart family is one of the original coal barons in West Virginia. Their money goes back a long time. I've been told that the remaining heirs have decided to move permanently to a place with palm trees and sandy beaches. Not a bad idea, huh?"

"That's a great idea. I'll probably do that myself one of these days," she replied as she cleaned up her desk. "Elroy brought in some things earlier today."

"Oh, did he? Sometimes I wonder about that boy," he said, shaking his head. "So what do you think about this Victorian bedroom set that I've got here? Do you have anyone who's seriously thinking of buying it?"

"No, not really. Of course, you never know when someone will come in from out of town and buy it. It's beautiful, and it looks great in here. People always ooh and aah over it. But for these higher-priced pieces, especially since you want to keep the set together, you'll do better with it by taking it to Texas. Sometimes I think that some of the people who come in here think they're just visiting another museum. The way they come in and just look around, browsing has become a national pastime."

"Well, I'll plan on taking it with me then. I'll bring the truck down one day next week and pick it up. I've got some Eastlake furniture that I'll bring here in its place so you won't have an empty space here."

"That's fine. Davy will help you to load and unload."

"You've done a fine job with those frames," he said, looking around the room.

"Thank you. I enjoy working on them. Even Belle has started doing some of them. I need to go out to your place one of these days sometime soon and pick up some more. I've only got a few left that we haven't restored. I'll give you a call first. Give you a warning."

"Well, since that's quite a little drive for you from here, if you ever do come out there and I'm not there for some reason, just get Marla to let you into the barn. You just go ahead and take the ones you want. We can always settle up later. I trust you. Now that's something that I haven't said to very many people."

"Thank you. I feel honored," Franny said with a smile. Then she saw a large pickup pull up in front of the store.

Ray, realizing that Franny was going to be busy, started to leave. "I know you do. Hey, I've got to be going. Tell Belle, when you see her, that I wish her God's blessings. See you later."

5

Just as Franny was going through the process of closing up the store for the day, a pickup pulled up and stopped in front of Johnson's. Franny was surprised to see that the driver of the truck was a beautiful girl with long brown hair who was very pregnant. The girl was relieved to see that Franny was still there.

"Hello. Are you the one that called this morning to ask if I would stay late for you?" Franny asked the young woman, who looked as if she were about to pop out her baby at any moment.

"Yes. I'm Beth Koch. Thank you. I appreciate you waiting for me."

Franny looked at each piece of furniture in the woman's truck and gave her a price on stripping and refinishing them. The woman agreed to the prices, and Franny told her to drive around to the back of the store to unload. Franny hurried through the building, picking up a receipt and a pen, hoping that Davy hadn't left yet and would be there to unload the truck.

No luck. Davy's truck was gone. He'd left to make a delivery of a baker's chest that he'd finished. The woman backed her pickup into the loading dock area.

"I don't know what I was thinking," said Franny.

I didn't think, she thought to herself.

"Belle's not here today, and Davy has left to make a delivery. I'm sorry, but I don't have anyone to help me unload all of this."

"No problem," said Beth. "I loaded it up, and I guess I can unload it."

"You loaded all of this by yourself? Oh my God! How far along are you?"

"A little over eight months. Hey, I've been a farm girl all of my life. This is nothing compared to the work I've done on the farm," she said, laughing at Franny's concerned look on her face. Beth easily unhooked the back end of the pickup, fully intending to unload the truck herself.

"Wait a minute while I get a screwdriver. It'll be easier if we take off the doors and the drawers out to make things lighter. Let's see. Maybe I can get up in the truck and hand them down to you. Is that okay with you?"

"Fine," said Beth as Franny squeezed herself up into the back of the truck with the screwdriver in her hand. The first piece was a heavily painted chifferobe. Unlike an armoire, a chifferobe had drawers plus space for hanging clothes. It was a heavy piece of furniture. She took off the doors, pulled out the drawers, and handed them down to Beth, who placed them inside the building. It was still heavy, but at least now it was a lot easier for her to hold onto the chifferobe as she gently slid it over the edge and down to Beth, who picked it up as if it were light as a feather and set it next to the other pieces.

Franny marveled at her strength. There were serpentine drawers on the walnut dresser and the chest of drawers. There was a walnut headboard and footboard of the bed to complete the set. Someone had hand-painted the whole set white with a colorful design to make it look more appealing for a young girl.

Beth seemed to enjoy the work of unloading the furniture. "This is going to be beautiful when you get it refinished."

"So was this your bedroom furniture when you were young?"

"No. We bought this at Rogers Flea Market up the river from East Liverpool."

"I know where you mean. I went there once last year. That place is unbelievable! I've never seen anything like it!" Franny remarked.

"You'd have to be there a week to see everything." Beth laughed.

Franny was glad when it was all unloaded and Beth had still not given birth to her child. She gave Beth a receipt for her furniture. "Take care, and I'll call you when it's ready, probably one week at the most."

"Good. It'll be ready before the baby gets here."

"I hope you're right. We can deliver your order for you, if you like?"

"No, thank you. I shouldn't have any problem. See you later. Bye."

"Good-bye." Franny quickly locked up the store, wrote a check for Belle for what was owed to her, and headed for Belle's house before going home.

Belle and her kids lived with her grandmother on a quiet, tree-lined street in an older neighborhood. Franny pulled into the driveway behind Belle's car. When no one answered when she knocked on the kitchen door, she slowly opened the door and softly called out "hello" as she entered the kitchen. The linoleum on the floor was so worn through with age that the pattern was worn off in places, but still clean enough to outshine any high-class kitchen.

She could see the children watching their television program in the living room as she took the hallway to their grandmother's bedroom, where Franny could see the old woman covered up to her chin with a blanket. All Franny could see of the small, elderly woman was that her African American face somehow seemed almost as pale as her white hair. Her eyes were closed in sleep.

Belle was sitting beside her bed with a full cup of soup in her hand that she'd tried to feed to her grandmother. She looked up as Franny entered the room. Belle was a small, dark-skinned, African American woman. The hard times she had suffered showed on her face. The father of her children was a come-and-go type of man she'd known since grade school. He'd promised many times that he would change his ways until his life got changed for him in the way of a drug overdose.

"Hey, good to see you," Belle said with a soft voice, not wanting to wake her grandmother.

"You too. How's she doing?"

Belle just shook her head. "Not good."

"Brought your paycheck," she said, handing it to her before sitting down in an old rocking chair. "Last week's pay plus your share of the picture frames and quilts."

"Thank you. We need this. We're about out of everything. Now I can go to the grocery store in the morning."

"Well, gotta get home and feed my cats. Davy and I are doing fine by ourselves at the store, so you take as much time as you need with your grandmother."

"My sister will be here next week to help out, so I'll be there Monday morning. I can't afford to miss too much time off work."

"Whatever you want to do is fine with me," Franny said as she got up to leave.

Belle walked with her to the kitchen door. "Thank you again for bringing the check."

"You're welcome. You earned it."

As she closed the kitchen door and walked to the car, she was thinking how much better life was now that she and Belle had bonded into a true friendship. She trusted her in every way, especially with the money.

6

The moment she stepped through the door from the garage to the basement, Franny knew that someone had been in her house. An overhead light that she would usually use before entering a small storage room to the right was on, and it shouldn't be. Her heart was racing, but also at the door, greeting her as usual, were two of her cats, Harry and Larry. It was a good sign that no one was in the basement, or else the cats would be in hiding.

She stood still, striving to remain calm, thinking back on her activities that morning, and trying to remember if she might've left the light on herself. She quietly opened the storage room door and looked in. Nothing was in there except the Christmas decorations and a couple miscellaneous boxes. She hadn't been in that room since she'd put away the Christmas things a few months ago.

Her heart was pounding while listening intently for any noise from above. This was an older house with floors that creaked and groaned from any movement that might come from above; however, the residence was quiet and still. Leaving the basement door open for a quick getaway, she cautiously walked through the basement and followed the two cats as they ran up the steps ahead of her to the kitchen. It was another good sign. They wouldn't go up there if someone were still in the house.

As quietly as the creaky floors would allow her, she searched through every room, the closets, and under the beds, including the one where her white cat, Rachel, her most jittery cat of them all, was peacefully sleeping. It appeared that nothing had been disturbed or was missing. However, a light she seldom used was on. She knew for sure that someone had been in her house.

Feeling violated and angry that someone had touched her things, she checked the doors and windows. Even the storm doors were still locked from the inside. Whoever it was must have come in through the garage because, coming in that way, he or she wouldn't have had to worry about her collie dog, Sunday, being able to get at him or her.

The only way that someone could get in that way would be if he or she had a garage-door opener with the same combination as hers. *What are the chances of that? Why would anyone even bother to come in here?* The television and stereo might bring a few dollars to someone, but they're still here. She had the feeling that something more sinister was in somebody's warped head. That would be the only reason why someone would take the time to find a way inside her home.

She filled the pet food bowls and put down fresh water inside the house for the cats. Then she went outside on the back porch and filled her beautiful, sable-colored collie's food and water bowl. Her previous owner, a collie breeder, had named her Sunday because that was the day of the week she was born on. He was not known to be a creative person. Franny decided to keep the name to help Sunday adjust to her new surroundings. Wagging her tail and giving her unconditional love, as she did to anyone with a kind aura, the dog waited for her traditional pat on the head and her ears rubbed before eating her food.

Later while showering to get off the smells of furniture stripper and refinishing materials, scrubbing even harder to get the filthy feeling of being violated, the thought of Michael crossed her mind. He loved to stir things up with people. Leaving the light on would be his way of messing with her mind, one of his favorite games.

Feeling a little better after showering and putting on fresh clothes, she noticed that the cats had also finished their after-dinner bathing and were now ready to go outside for the night. The two she called the twins, Harry and Larry, were beautiful and sweet with medium-length, light gray fur with white chests and stomach areas. Each had a streak of white on opposite sides of their mouths, a mirror image of each other. Petting them to remind them that they had a loving home to come back to, she let them go outside to hunt in the woods behind her house.

After washing her hands, she went next door to visit her neighbor, Simon, a professor of fine arts at a local university. He had a workshop set up in the basement of his home, where he created beautiful pottery. Of course, he was a few years younger than she was, which seemed to be true for anyone for whom she might be interested. He was one of the few good friends she had made since she returned to the area after having been gone for nearly twenty-five years. Now most of her family members that had once lived in the area had either died or moved away.

Simon was an attractive man of medium height with a slender build. Actually he was quite thin because he usually forgot to eat anything while working on his pottery. He had a long, light brown ponytail and a short, well-trimmed beard. She liked Simon because he was honest and sincere and not afraid to show the vulnerable and tender sides of himself.

After knocking on the door to his basement workshop, she called "hello" as she stepped inside. The pervading smell of fresh clay permeated the air. He was sitting at his worktable, using a magnifying lamp, looking for any imperfections in a beautiful vase that he'd recently removed from the kiln.

"Hey, Franny. How're you doing?" he asked with his usual broad smile and perky attitude.

She never understood how he could always be so cheerful. He was probably one of those pleasant babies who every mother loved to call their own.

"Fine," she said. "Except someone's been in my house while I was gone today."

"No kidding? What happened? Did they take anything? Did you call the police?" he asked in a very concerned way.

She explained to him about the light that was on in the basement. "No. I didn't call the police. They'd just think I was crazy. I don't think anything is missing. Anyway, nothing that's noticeable."

All of the emotion that had built up over the past hour was now released full blast onto Simon, who wisely allowed her to vent as he nodded his head in sympathy.

"I know that light was not on when I went to work this morning. I pass right under it while going to the garage. I can't believe that someone would take the time to break into my home. I've traveled and lived halfway around the world. Nothing like this has ever happened to me. I come home to a nice small town where you should feel safer, and somebody breaks into my house! It's unbelievable! I just showered, and I still feel dirty and violated. You know? Somebody touched my stuff! I'd like to know just who in the hell they think they are!"

All the while, she was pacing back and forth in front of his worktable. Dejectedly, she sat down on a stool across from him. "I do feel fortunate that nothing seems to be missing and no one was there when I got home."

"That's one good thing. Do you have any ideas whom it might have been?"

"Not really. I don't even know very many around here anymore. I see a lot of people at work, but I can't imagine any of them doing something like this. The only weird person I know is Michael, and you know how he is. That guy's a real sociopath, meaning that everything he does is okay as long as it fills his needs. I think he enjoys playing with people's minds too much to be dangerous. At least that's what I keep telling myself."

"Yea. He's one for the books all right." Simon started cleaning up his work area.

"The only way I can see that anyone might have gotten in is through the garage. So I was wondering if you would change the combination on the garage door for me."

"Sure, no problem. I'll do it right now," said Simon. "I need to take a break now anyway."

They went to the garage. She got her light aluminum ladder so he could reach the opener mechanism.

As he stood on the ladder, he said, "You know, Franny, you have a bad habit of not always locking your car. You need to think about getting into that habit."

"I know," she said, looking up at him while holding the ladder steady for him.

When he finished changing the combination, they went to The Tavern, one of the favorite restaurants in the area, for some dinner and a beer. Simon was currently between girlfriends. His relationships with girls didn't last long. They usually got tired of waiting for him to finish up whatever he was working on so they could go out and do something, like have some fun. After a while of being patient and then impatient, they usually just drifted off, usually with no hard feelings, just disgusted with themselves for having wasted their time. Franny told him that someday he'd find someone who would appreciate just knowing that he was there.

The Tavern's food was excellent with a pleasant atmosphere. One entrance of the restaurant took one into the area that had upholstered booths on the left and a bar on the right. Another door took someone into an area primarily used for pleasant dining without having to put up with the vulgarities from those at the bar.

They chose the bar side, as usual, and entered. Several men were seated at the bar, all scrubbed clean of coal dust from the mines, dirt from the local steel mill, or wherever. There were only two empty booths. They selected one and sat down.

"Well," said Simon as he looked over the menu, "I've known Michael for a lot of years. We lived up the road from his family when we were kids. He was always a little strange, in addition to being a liar and a thief. I hate seeing you working with him."

"Yea. I know. But it's so hard to find a decent job around here, and the fact is that I do enjoy my job. Another thing is that his parents, Richard and Sara, have become good friends to me. When Richard had his stroke, he gave management of the store to me and not Michael. Which, of course, Michael had a fit over that for a long time. Life was definitely quite difficult for me there for a while. But now that his home inspections business is doing well, things are starting to smooth over a bit. It's gotten a little easier for us to work together. Another thing is, although he hasn't said anything to me, of course, I think he's cut back on his drinking."

"It would be good if he did. Although I know he's had a hard life, drinking doesn't make things any easier. His parents seem like fine people now, but they weren't always that way," said Simon. "My folks told me that, when Michael was young, they gave him a rough time. His mother didn't feel like being a mother until his younger brother, Richard Jr., came along. Then they got religion and changed their lives around for the better. Junior became the light of his parent's lives, but it was too late for them to make a difference with Michael. He resented it all, especially them being such good parents to Richard Jr. With all of the love and attention he received, he grew up being a well-adjusted and happy kid. Which proves the theory that, if you raise a kid with plenty of love and kindness, instead of beating him all of the time for no reason at all, he'll probably turn out to be a pretty good person."

"I've heard that said about them before, that Michael was more or less just a nuisance to them when they were younger. Thank God most people mellow out in their older age. I guess we're all guilty of having made mistakes when we were younger. I just know them the way they are now. They're good to me. I like working for them."

"Oh! Oh!" Simon said in a low voice. Then he smiled broadly and said hello to a woman who was with two other women. She returned his greeting and stiffly passed on to a booth down from theirs.

"An ex-girlfriend," he said in a matter-of-fact way. "We had a good time for a while. Then she became a little too demanding. She couldn't understand that, when I'm busy trying to get enough products ready for an upcoming show, I just can't drop everything and go out partying. If you don't have a good presentation at these shows, you don't get invited to the next one they have. Spending my off-work hours in a free and creative way is very important to me. I'm not going to let anyone take away one of my life's greatest pleasures. It just won't happen. Besides, doing these shows will count a great deal toward me receiving tenure at the university, which is coming up the end of this next school year."

"Well, someday the right one will come along for you. I've pretty much resigned myself to the idea that I'll be traveling this lifetime alone. But I'm not complaining. I've had a good life. I've traveled to faraway places while in the navy, which was a childhood dream. I attended the local colleges where I was stationed, seven colleges in all, finally graduating from Wheeling Jesuit University. And now I'm learning the antique business. Sometimes I feel that I've come to this planet on a learning expedition. With my little family of pets, I feel I'm probably just as happy as anyone else is, just the way my life is right now. I'd have to say that I haven't seen anyone yet that I would ever want to trade places with, no matter how much fame or fortune they have to keep them comfortable."

"You can always count on me for friendship," said Simon. "You're one of the best friends I've ever had." Seeing the astonished look on her face, he added, "I mean it! You're someone intelligent to talk to, and you don't whine about anything. I feel that I can talk to you about anything. That's important to me."

Franny was smiling, pleased to hear Simon's comments about her.

"And besides, you just never know when someone special will come into your life. Especially since you do meet a lot of people at the antique store."

"Yes, I know. The problem is that I'm the type of person who is just a little overly sensitive about things. I can drive somebody crazy in no time at all."

"Oh, I find that hard to believe," said Simon.

"It's true. I'll never again put up with someone who isn't a sensitive person, not only other people's feelings but also anything with the molecules of life. That includes other animals and things like snakes, fish, plants, trees, and even rocks." She laughed. "The type who would feel the pain to the rose bush when its flowers are cut or the stress a fish feels when it's yanked out of the water. Things like that. That's not asking too much of someone, is it?"

Simon laughed with her as the waitress arrived to take their orders.

With that accomplished, Franny went on to say, "Of course, I'm not saying that people shouldn't fish or cut flowers. Just have enough respect to feel that moment of stress with them and appreciate what they're giving up for us."

"I've never thought of things like that before I met you. Like most people, I've just gone through life taking everything for granted without a thought for the life around us."

"And let's see," she went on. "It would have to be someone who feels the power of being a part of the universe, not just a part of a family, town, or church, but the whole universe. It would have to be a very sensitive and caring person, an enlightened, civilized person. And believe me. They're rare." She laughed. "I know that's a lot to ask for, but that's what I require."

"You deserve someone like that, just what you want from someone. I have to tell you that, after being around you for these past few years, I understand why I've never been happy with the women I've been with in the past. I think I want some of those same requirements that you have. I'm so tired of dating girls whose concern in life is their weight or how their hair looks. Their goal in life is to snag any man as long as he isn't too mouthy and he looks good in jeans. I want someone with a lot more depth to their character than that. I've had enough of those other types of women."

After finishing their meal and relaxing with a beer, they listened to the jukebox for a while and then had another beer.

Later arriving at home, Franny wished she could call Belle and talk to her about what had happened, that someone had been in her house. Belle was so strong. She just naturally exuded an air of understanding and strength that made most problems seem so much easier to handle. But it was late, and Belle was already loaded down with troubles of her own. The last thing she needed was something else to worry about.

Instead Franny turned on the television to the local news. A young female news reporter was doing a special report on strange happenings in the tri-state area. "It seems," she said, "that another person living alone has been found dead in his home, the fourth one in the past two months. The most recent one being an older man by the name of George Popka, found dead in his home this past Saturday morning. Killed with a blunt instrument to the back of his head. Robbery seems to be the reason for these murders. Police are investigating the possibility that these murders are connected in some way. We ask that all of our viewers be a little more cautious about whom you let into your home. We will continue to update you with this story as more information is gathered. Stay tuned into WTRF-TV7, the Valley's favorite news station."

Umm, thought Franny, *this is all getting too creepy.* She brought in Sunday to spend the night. Although she hated the smell of a dog in the house, she'd rather put up with the odor to feel safe and get a good night's rest.

Franny finally drifted off to sleep that night with the smell of dog drifting up from where Sunday was sleeping on the floor beside her bed, thinking that it was past time for the collie to have a bath.

7

In the morning, the birds were singing joyously, loud and clear, their way of repaying her for all that birdseed she fed them throughout the past winter. Franny forced herself out of bed to turn off the alarm before it went off. That was a sound that she couldn't stand to hear.

Looking into the other bedroom, she saw Sunday still sleeping beside the empty bed. It was bad when even your dog sleeps in the other bedroom.

"Come on, Sunday. Time to go outside."

As she admired her beautiful coat, which was similar to the famous collie Lassie, she opened the kitchen door to let Sunday outside for her morning constitutional and the cats, Harry, Larry, and Rachel, in from their night of prowling. The cats finished eating their breakfast and then climbed up on her still warm bed and settled comfortably for a peaceful sleep while she got ready for work. She was just about to leave when the telephone rang. She picked up the receiver before she even spoke.

She heard a very low and soft voice say, "Franny." It was Belle.

"Good morning," she replied. "How's your grandmother doing?"

"The same, not very good at all. I hate to leave her, but I just can't afford to miss any more days of work. Some of the churchwomen came over last night, and they have volunteered to help out, starting today. Also Mrs. Jackson, the woman who lives next door, is going to look in on her during the day whenever the women from church might not be able to be here. Grandma knows these women, and I think she'll feel comfortable with them. She's been sleeping most of the time now. They told me that she might linger for several weeks, and since I need the money, I should let them help out and get back to work. I am so relieved that they're going to help us. They are a real blessing. Now would you believe that my car won't start? Would you please stop by for me this morning?"

"Sure, no problem. I'll be leaving in just a few minutes, so I'll be there shortly."

"Great. I'll be looking for you. Thanks, Franny."

Belle lived just a couple miles away from where Franny did, so picking her up to go to work did not put her out of her way by very much. Years ago, their families had lived on the same street. Belle's grandmother's house was about the halfway point between the grocery store and Franny's home. Franny continued her mother's habit when she was old enough to go for the family's groceries. She would stop and rest a few moments and visit with Belle's great-grandmother as she sat on the front porch swing. She remembered the time when, as a little girl, she had fallen, badly scraping her knees.

The gentle, young black man, who later became Belle's father, not yet out of high school, called to her, asking if she were okay. He had knelt down, picked her up, and gently carried her up the hill to her home. She recalled the surprised but grateful look on her mother's face when she answered the door, seeing the tall, black man holding her little girl in his arms.

As she drove down Belle's street, she could see her waiting by her thirteen-year-old Chevy, which had been dying of old age for quite some time now. Proud of her African heritage, Belle had various parts of her hair in stylish corn rolls. She was in a very colorful and attractive top and blue jeans. She not only dressed up herself, but she also helped to dress up Johnson's. Her job at the store was primarily sales, so she was quite often much better dressed than Franny was. Since Belle spent almost all of her money on her children, she shopped for herself at the House of the Carpenter in Wheeling, a Salvation Army-type of place. Thankfully, when the more affluent women in this area gained weight, they'd take their almost new clothes to the House of the Carpenter in Wheeling, where they'd sell them to those less fortunate for only a few dollars.

Of course, Belle's three children, all teenagers now, would never think of wearing something from there. They had to have Tommy Hilfiger brand clothes or some other popular brand. Especially when it came to her oldest son, Eddy, who was constantly in trouble with the police. She had bought him all of the expensive clothes, CDs, PlayStation, or anything to win him back from the gang that she thought controlled him. It was clear as could be to everyone else that, now that the older gang members had been put in jail, Eddy was the one who was the head of the remaining gang members. Everyone knew that Belle would never believe that of her son, even if someone had the courage to tell her. All one could do was watch her suffer and be her friend when she let you.

"Ohhh, God! You wouldn't believe what I've been through already this morning," said Belle. "The police were pounding on my door at six o'clock this morning, looking for Eddy as usual. And don't you know? When he heard them pounding on the door, that idiot ran down and tried to hide in the basement. I just stood there and let them look for him. What else could I do? They'd find him eventually. It isn't like they were going to just forget about him."

Belle kept on talking as if she had to get it all out of her system as quickly as possible, "Luckily Grandma didn't understand what the commotion was all about. She thinks it was just Eddy and some of his friends being too loud. She thinks that Eddy is the greatest grandson that a woman could ever have. It'll break her heart to find out that he's in trouble again. Hopefully I can keep that from her."

"What did he do now?"

"He and those idiot friends of his broke into someone's basement and stole a bunch of stuff. They're too lazy to leave the neighborhood to commit their crimes. Just one more reason for the neighbors to want us out of here. A couple of the neighbors already treat us like trash because of him and his friends.

"I was already a nervous wreck after they took Eddie to the detention center and taking care of Grandma. But I'm determined not to miss work because of him. It's not fair to the girls to never have money for them. So of course, when I tried to start my car, it wouldn't turn over. I don't know what I'm going to do about that," she said with exasperation.

"I can't imagine how you manage to keep going with all the troubles in your life. Kids are so hard to deal with these days. They don't understand how much you love them, and that's a shame. Yours act like they each want you to show them just how much of a sacrifice you'll make for them."

"That's it exactly."

Arriving at the store for the beginning of the day's work was a blessing for them both. Belle and Franny both enjoyed working with most of the people who came into Johnson's. For Belle, not only was it a way to earn a living, it was also a place to put her problems aside for a while and work at a job she enjoyed. She was proud of the partnership that she and Franny had formed. Now she had hope that their financial difficulties would eventually end.

However, what she had once thought of the bad years was nothing compared to these years. Her oldest son Eddy was hooked on drugs and alcohol. He had been home for only two months after spending the previous twelve months locked up at a boy's facility. Now it looked as though he'd be going back for another eighteen months. He was her firstborn, her baby. How would she ever bear it! Now her grandmother, in her early eighties, was in her last days. Her parents passed away years ago, her father from heart disease and her mother from diabetes.

For Franny, the job at Johnson's gave her a stated position in life. When she was in the navy, she enjoyed having her rank on her sleeve and the number of years that she had served. All could see this and show each other the proper respect. That was one of her most difficult problems to overcome the first few years after retiring from twenty years with the navy.

People didn't look at her with respect anymore, and she no longer had anyone to look up to with respect. People just went about their business, not really noticing anyone. Except, of course, women were noticed for their looks only, not that she ever wanted to be classified in with those. At her age now, it was mostly much older men who looked at her that way, which was disgusting to her. However, she did get the occasional younger man eyeing her.

Now she was the manager of Johnson's, not really a great position for most people, but it was all she needed to feel that she belonged someplace in this world. It was a great feeling to enjoy one's job and have respect for oneself. At work, she never knew what was going to happen from one minute to the next or who was going to walk in the door or call on the phone, just like it was in the navy.

She drove past the store before making a right turn into the parking lot in the rear. She saw that someone had left the filthiest and ugliest Hoosier chest that she had ever seen sitting right in front of the door. Whoever left it there probably had no worry that anyone would steal it in its present condition. People would buy all sorts of filthy things at yard sales or auctions and bring it to the antique store in the same condition it was bought. Of course, they never thought to clean anything before bringing it to Johnson's. Ewww! She hated to touch it to move it back a little so she could unlock the door.

With Belle's help, they dragged both pieces of the chest inside and placed it to the side. Davy would take it into the back when he came in. She went on back through to the rear of the building, turning on the lights as she went. She had noticed while coming through the back entrance that Michael's chest was not there. Well, maybe he came back later and took it home with him to work on in his garage.

He did that sometimes, so she was not too concerned that it was no longer there. Maybe Davy helped him to load it up last night after they delivered the armoire to Joanna.

After opening the store for business and while placing the display items outside, Franny saw that Michael had brought a colorful reproduction carousel horse. She dragged that outside to attract attention and improve the look of the store. *This should catch people's eyes,* she thought to herself.

"Hel-Hello. Wh-What's going on?" Jerry asked as he came into the store and started looking around as if he were looking for something. "Th-th-that's junk! P-p-piece of junk! Wh-wh-where'd you get that horse?"

"I think Michael brought it here last night."

"W-W-Well, I-I-I'll b-b-be! D-ding-dong's here!" he said, noticing Belle getting the cash register ready for the day. "H-How's your grandmother doing?"

"Not good."

"Sorry to hear that."

"Me too," said Davy as he came into the showroom area and set down his thermos of coffee.

Davy was originally from South Carolina and still had a soft Southern accent. He never seemed to notice when others appraised him as a very handsome man. His wife was from this area and had met Davy while visiting some relatives in his hometown in South Carolina. They were both young, and sometimes their relationship became quite strained, which was probably not unusual for young marriages.

"Good morning, Davy. I don't see Michael's chest here. Did you help him load it up last night?

"No," said Davy as he started toward the back to look around the room for the chest.

"We unloaded that carousel horse and then loaded the armoire and delivered it to Joanna. After we delivered the armoire at Joanna's, he dropped me off here and drove off. I just got in my truck and went home. He didn't say anything to me about wanting to take the chest anywhere. It was here when we left with the armoire. Joanna had us sit that armoire four different places before she finally decided where she wanted to leave it sitting."

"Well, with a large piece of furniture like that, it makes a difference in the balance of a room," said Franny. "Also I have the feeling that she's one of those women who has the added fear of not having something just perfect to please her husband."

"I'd thrown out that old drunk a long time ago," said Belle.

"You'll never guess what happened to me last night," Franny said to Belle and Davy.

"What?" asked Davy.

"Somebody was in my house while I was at work yesterday."

Belle's jaw dropped down, and her eyes grew wide with concern.

"No kidding. Did they take anything?" he asked.

"Nothing that I could see." Then she told them the story about the light being on when it should not have been. Also she told them about Simon changing the code for the garage door.

"Well, that's so weird," said Belle.

Davy nodded his head in agreement. "Did you call the police?"

"No, they'll probably just think that I'm crazy or something," said Franny.

After taking the ugly-looking Hoosier to the back with the other painted furniture, Davy put paint stripper on it to let soak through about ten layers of paint. Then he took a piece of furniture that belonged to the same order as the piece that Franny was working on and set it near Franny so they could work together. That refinish order included the secretary, a curio chest, and a small table. All of the pieces of this order were repaired and stripped clean of old dirt and varnish. So now they would sand them down until they felt soft and smooth. Then they'd wash them down with mineral spirits that dried within a few minutes. After drying, they would wipe them down with a sticky tack cloth to clean any little pieces of dirt that might still be on the piece. The order called for a natural finish, so no stain was needed, especially for this type of wood, a beautiful red oak. It was a thrill to see the wood instantly change from a bland, colorless look to its beautiful natural coloring. The pieces would have to dry for at least two hours before another coat of polyurethane could be applied.

"Davy, before you start anything else, while these are drying and setting up, I was wondering if you would go and see if you can get Belle's car running for her."

"Sure," said Davy. "I'll go and get her keys."

"You can take the store van. Call me if you think it needs any new parts."

The telephone started ringing. "Johnson's Antique Store," she answered.

"Howdy," said the voice on the other end. "This is Allen. I'm a friend of Michael's. We met the other day."

"I remember," said Franny.

From the sound of his voice, a picture of a whiskey-swigging Allen with a cigar sticking out of his mouth passed through her mind.

"I left that Hoosier chest outside your door this morning. It's a little rough, but I think it'll clean up all right. I just want the paint stripped off it. I'll finish it up myself. When do you think it'll be ready for me to pick up?"

"Give me a week, just to be sure," she said.

"Okay," said Allen. "I'll be in touch." He hung up before she could ask him for a telephone number in case she needed to call him.

"He sounded drunk," she said as she hung up the phone.

"Hello," a soft voice floated to where they were working. It was Joanna, walking in from the front area. "Just stopped by to let you how much I love my armoire," she said with a big smile. This meant that she as well as her husband loved the armoire. "Please stop by sometime when you can. I want you to see how it looks in our guest room."

"That's great! That is a beautiful armoire. It has been well taken care of, and now you'll take even better care of it. It has found a good home," said Franny.

"Thank you. Have to run. I just wanted to stop by and tell you how pleased I am with the armoire. I'm meeting my sister to go shopping."

Joanna's sister Marilyn was the only one other than her husband that she ever spent any time with, and he was seldom home, staying out late at night at the bars. Her days were usually spent alone, writing romance novels. Outside of her family, Franny was the only other one in town who knew that Joanna was a writer. Joanna had autographed her latest and given it to Franny as a gift. Franny would keep Joanna's life as a romance novelist a secret.

Davy had returned while Franny was talking to Joanna. And when Joanna left, Belle walked over to Franny with a big smile on her face.

"Davy said that all my car needs is for me to add dry gas each time I fill up the tank. That'll keep water from collecting in the distributor, which is why it wouldn't start this morning. What a relief! I was afraid that it was going to be something much worse and more expensive than that. Thank you, Franny, for letting Davy go and take care of that for me."

"You're welcome. There was no need for you to have to worry about that in addition to all of the other things you have to be concerned about. I'm glad that it's nothing serious."

They went through a three-hour rush period. Franny could never understand why it usually happened like that. People coming in to drop things off for refinishing or to pick things up that were finished always seemed to come and go at the same time. Belle was kept busy up front with customers looking to buy. Whether they bought anything or not, she would first have to listen to their stories of furniture someone in their family had and the condition it was in when they last saw it.

It wasn't until later in the afternoon when Michael stopped into the store. He had parked his van in the back of the building and walked through to where Franny and Davy were working.

"Where's my chest?"

"We don't know. We thought that you must have taken it last night."

"I didn't take it! What'd you do with it?" His voice was rising toward a shout.

"We didn't do anything with it. It was gone when we came into work this morning," Franny said in a calm voice.

"Who was in here? Who could have taken it? That chest is from the early eighteen hundreds," he said as he tried to maintain control of himself. "That is a very valuable chest!"

"Well, I have no idea who might have taken it. Everything was locked up as usual when I came in this morning. It doesn't look like anything else is missing. All we can do is report it to the police."

"Oh! I can't believe this!" Michael fumed. He was now walking back and forth in front of their work area. He was visibly very upset as he went over in his mind the events of the past few days. He was trying to think of who might have even known that he had the chest.

"Do you want me to call the police to at least file a report?"

That was a good question because antique dealers liked to keep their business to themselves, especially dealers like Michael. It was rare that anyone ever got the best of him. This was an outrage to him personally.

"No. I don't want anyone to know that something's been stolen from here. That would be bad for business for all of us. Change the locks on the doors, front and back. Don't say anything to anyone about this. I'll find out who took that chest." He walked back through the way that he had come in and left.

Franny called the locksmith to come over right away and change the locks. Late in the afternoon, a pickup truckload of the heavily painted woodwork, including a staircase with one hundred and fifty spindles, and two mantels arrived, filling the whole back loading dock area.

"I'll call Kevin and Joey to come in on Saturday to help you strip all of that painted woodwork."

This was their second year working for Johnson's. They were high-school seniors this year and enjoyed working there whenever they were needed. Teenagers always needed more money. They also liked the idea that they were doing a man's work with decent pay, not like their friends who worked at the fast-food places for minimum wage.

"Okay. I'll be here," said Davy.

"Hel-Hello. Wh-What's going on?" Jerry asked as he came in the work area and started looking around. "Th-Tha's junk! P-Piece of junk!"

"Yeah, and you wish that junk was yours." She got his box of keys and gave them to him. "Thanks for the keys. We did find one that works."

"K-Keep that one. I've g-got a lot more keys like that at home," said Jerry.

"Thank you. I'm sure these people will be happy to have a key for their china chest."

They heard the bell coming from the front of the store. It was Margaret, who had one of the rental spaces there, and with her was her best friend, her daughter-in-law Ann. Now nearing the age of seventy, Margaret stayed young and happy, keeping busy with her antique business.

Thanks to the help of Ann and Johnson's, the two of them loved to go to auctions together and thought nothing of traveling long distances for auctions. Beautiful and valuable antiques filled both of their homes.

"Hey! Hello!" They called out at the same time in their exuberance to say hello.

"Look at this over here, Margaret," said Ann.

They were looking at a beautiful walnut, Victorian bedroom set that another renter, Ray Rouse, had brought in since the last time they were there. The set included a dresser with a handkerchief box on either side of the marble top. The mirror had a two-inch bevel and was beautifully framed with walnut wood. The matching headboard and footboard for the bed had a plain but beautiful design. The dry sink had a marble top that matched the dresser top. Margaret's favorite period was the Victorian, so she was in awe of such a beautiful set.

"We were passing by this way, so we thought we'd drop in and see what's going on in here today." Ann was always like a ray of sunshine that had come into the room. By this time, stuttering Jerry has joined them in the front. "Hi, Jerry," said Ann.

"H-hi," said Jerry. "Ar-are you ladies going to the B-Barnhart auction? T-that's a week from this Saturday. I-I got this listing right here if you want to look at it. Everybody'll be at that one." He held out the listing for Ann to look over.

"Look," said Ann. She showed the listing to Margaret. "We've been talking about going to this one; however, it's a bit of a drive from here. We have a beautiful state, but these winding roads of West Virginia get to be a bit tiresome. Hmmm. There probably will be a good turnout for this. We might go. What do you think, Margaret?"

"Fine with me. Whatever you think, I'm just the passenger." She laughed. "It does look like it has an excellent selection of Victorian pieces." She handed the listing back to Jerry.

"By the way," said Franny as she handed Margaret a check for a couple lamps that were sold, "did you hear on the news last night about that man being murdered?"

"Yes," said Ann. "Margaret and I were talking about that earlier. We were wondering just what is going on with that. Such a shame. Those poor people all alone and probably not able to defend themselves."

"The sad thing is that they live alone until the day they die, and then relatives come out of the woodwork to claim anything they can get from them," said Margaret.

"W-well. P-people ha-have always been like that. They don't care. I-I've got to go. I-I'll be seeing you out at the auction," said Jerry as he waved good-bye and took his leave.

"We have to be going too," said Ann. "I have to get Margaret home so she can rest up for dinner. We've been running around all day, and I know that I'm tired, so you probably are too, Margaret." She took Margaret's arm. "Come and visit us sometime soon."

"Yes. I'll be stopping by sometime soon. I'll call and warn you first. I'm glad you stopped in. It's always nice to see you both. Good-bye."

"See ya. Good-bye," they said as they left the store for Ann's new Ford pickup.

Franny went back and worked with Davy for the remainder of the workday. He told her about the latest episode with his wife and her alcohol and drug problems. Just when he thought that she was going to straighten out, he'd go home to find her high on something. Now she seemed to be hooked on the drug Ecstasy. It was a good thing that her parents helped take care of the children.

Later that night, lying awake in bed, all sorts of thoughts entered Franny's head. *What if the person who entered my house thought I had valuable antiques? Maybe they had seen me buy something when I was representing Michael at a sale that he couldn't attend himself and had asked me to buy some particular thing for him. That's very possible. Or since I work at Johnson's, maybe someone thinks, quite naturally, that I would have antiques at home. They wanted to see what I had. Or maybe it was Michael. Maybe someone told him that I had bought something that I didn't. He doesn't trust anyone. Maybe he wanted to see just what I had here. Maybe he took his chest. That is not unlike something that he might do. Oh! This could drive a person crazy. Maybe I should call Chief Tenner in the morning.* She knew him from her high-school days. *I'll see what he says.*

Just as she was about to fall asleep, a light bulb went on in her head. She jumped up out of bed and went to the kitchen. The keys to the store were not hanging where they should have been.

"Oh no! Michael will kill me!"

It's a good thing I changed the locks today, she thought. *Oh no! Another sleepless night with the stinky dog odor drifting over my bed.*

"Tomorrow, I'm making an appointment for you to get a bath!"

Sunday just looked at her as if to say, "I hope this is nothing serious?"

After getting dressed the next morning, she called Chief Stan Tenner.

"Hey, how you doing?" He knew it was her.

As soon as she said his name, it caused her to wonder what kind of odd voice she might have for him to recognize her that quickly. She told him about the light being on in her basement at home the night before last and said the extra keys to Johnson's were missing.

"Come on down, and we'll fill out a report," said Stan. "I don't know if you've been listening to the news or not, but we've been having some bad stuff going on in the area. It'd be a good idea, just to be on the safe side, mind you, that I come up and check this over for you."

8

When she got to work, she told Belle and Davy about the keys that were missing from her house. Their eyes grew large as they realized the enormity of what she was saying. "And that's how they were able to get in and take Michael's chest."

"Oh my God!" Davy said. "Somebody was in your house!"

"Well, yes. Didn't you believe me?"

"Well, it seemed like such an outrageous thing for someone to do that I think that we didn't want to believe it was true. We thought that maybe you had forgotten that you'd left it on yourself," said Belle. "But, Lord, this is something! Who knows what this person could've done to you!"

"You're lucky that this person wasn't there when you got home. I think it must be someone who knows you, someone who comes in here. Don't you think?"

"It has to be," said Belle. "Now I'm going to be suspicious of everyone who usually comes in here."

"It might not be someone who comes in here," said Franny. "A lot of people, especially other dealers, know Michael and the setup we have here. It might be someone who knew that he bought that chest and brought it here. It could be anyone."

"That's true," said Davy. "Just the same though, we need to keep an eye on people when they come in here. Especially that Jerry Manning.

That guy's so nervous that he gets my nerves in a jangle after just being around him for a few minutes."

"Mine too, but if we throw him out, he'll just complain to Mr. Johnson, and he'll just let him back in again. Well, I guess we'd better get to it here. We've got a lot to get done today."

The phone rang, and another busy day got started.

A little later in the morning, Michael came in, looking all gloomy. Most people couldn't stand for someone to get the better of them, and Michael was no exception.

However, Franny knew she had to tell him about the keys. "Michael, I've realized that something was missing from my house the other day."

"What's missing?" he asked.

"My extra set of keys to the store."

Steam seemed to roll out of his ears as he tried to control himself.

"It's a good thing that we did go ahead and change the locks," she went on, trying not to notice him struggling to control his anger.

"Well, that explains how they got in to take the chest," he said in a low voice.

She didn't expect him to take it so easily. Maybe they were making headway in their relationship. He looked over a piece of furniture that he was planning to take to Georgia in a few weeks. Then he left without saying another word.

Franny started working on a picture frame that she had gotten from Ray Rouse. Ray had every size frame imaginable in his barn. It was always hard for her to decide which ones to buy from him. She was beginning to think that he was saving them for her since his supply only lessened by the ones she bought from him. She tried to think of other things while she worked. However, the fact that someone who knew her broke into her home, touched her things, and invaded her private world made her feel violated, defenseless, and dirty.

Marge Fodor, the glass lady, as people referred to her, came in during the afternoon. Belle helped her to carry in glassware from her car. She'd brought in several pieces of glass to replace those that were sold. Several older ladies from a tour group happened to come in at the same time. They immediately became interested in Marge's glassware, making it difficult to get the glass put away on the shelves. One of them did end up buying a salt and pepper shaker from her. Franny wrote a check for the amount due her for some other items that Belle had sold for her. She also gave her an itemized listing of the glassware sold.

"I got these in Moundsville the other night," said Marge, holding up a couple of beautiful Fostoria bowls that had been made at the local Fostoria glass factory that used to be in Moundsville, West Virginia, about ten miles south of Wheeling.

Franny added those, as well as the other items she just brought in, to Marge's inventory list.

"They're beautiful," said Belle. "It's a shame that the local glass factories are no longer in business. It's amazing to know that our local area produced such beautiful works of art."

"I was wondering if you two have heard about the Victorian mall that they're going to be putting in. The way I understand it, the mall will be right here next to the Center Market."

"That's the way I understand it. Of course, everything is still on the drawing board. It'll be a while before it becomes a reality."

"Oh, I hope so," said Marge. "Business in this area will pick up for everyone once that gets set up. I have been doing so much better since I've set up here in Johnson's, especially now that Belle works full time." She gave Belle a hug and a pat on the back. "You work miracles for us here, Belle, and I thank you."

"We're all glad to have Belle here," said Franny.

"Okay! That's enough," said Belle. "I'm just happy to have a job I like and that pays me halfway decently." Belle was embarrassed because some potential customers had come in and were looking around the store.

"We just wanted to let you know that we love you," Franny said with a smile as Belle rolled her eyes at them, even though she appreciated that they were trying to lift her spirits. She went over to see if she could be of help to the people who had come in and were looking around.

"See you girls next week, and thank you," said Marge as she left the store.

Later, after she went home to look after her animals, Franny went to the police station to file her statement.

The deputy handed her a form to fill out. "Chief said he's expecting you to stop by the house for some dinner. They'll be waiting for you."

Franny squished her face in a show of agony and left for the chief's house.

"Hey, Stan."

He held tightly onto the large German shepherd, Tara, as she tried to squeeze past them to get past the doorway area. Franny thought she was probably the only guest they'd had since acquiring the dog. The dog was straining to get closer to her as he noisily sniffed her legs.

"Finally, you made it here. Good to see you. Mary Lou's out in the kitchen."

"Smells delicious," Franny said as she made her way to the kitchen. The dog was close on her heels.

"Okay, Tara. That's enough. Go lay down." Franny was happy to see the dog go and lay down on the other side of the living room. "Now she knows that you're supposed to be here. She won't bother you."

"That's a relief!"

"Welcome," said Mary Lou as Franny entered the kitchen with its warm and comforting smell of homemade bread and spaghetti.

"That smells so good. I love spaghetti. Anything I can do to help?"

"Glad to hear that you love it. I was hoping you would. Have a seat in the living room with Stan. You must be tired. Just about ready to serve."

"So glad you were able to come to dinner. Tell me again about this break-in at your house and the store."

Franny went over the details once again, repeating that she had no idea who could have done such a thing. "However, just between you and me, since Michael didn't want the missing chest reported, I do have my suspicions. It's possible, since he is a devious kind of guy, that he took the keys and the chest himself."

"Why on earth would he do something like that?"

"He might want to make his father think I'm not responsible enough or capable in some way to keep Johnson's a safe place for people to bring their antiques. He may still be sore about my being the manager there instead of him. I don't know. It's just a thought to keep in mind."

"I hope that isn't true. However, you do need to be careful with Michael and anyone else who comes around there. I mean, don't be there by yourself. You can't trust anyone anymore. The word is out that they believe someone is murdering people who make purchases of high-value items at antique auctions and estate sales. Several states are included in this alert. Of course, now the FBI is involved."

"Wow! That's pretty scary."

"You bet it is. You need to take it serious."

"Dinner's ready," called Mary Lou. She then went to the upstairs stairway and called to their fifteen-year-old daughter Paula.

They immediately heard footsteps overhead and bounding down the stairs.

"Hi, Franny," she said with exuberance as Franny and Stan joined her at the table.

The conversation was lighthearted as they enjoyed the delicious meal.

"So good, Mary Lou. You could win a prize. I'll help you clean up."

"No, thank you. I spend all day sitting at a desk." Mary Lou was a secretary at an attorney's office. "I need to get up and move around a bit. Stan wants you to look at his old fire alarm boxes downstairs."

"Follow me," said Stan.

She followed him downstairs to the basement. After turning on the light, she followed him into a small room.

"These darn things have been in here for several years. When there was no need for them anymore, modernization you know, the city was just going to take them to the town dump. For some reason, I hated to see that happen, so I brought them here, and they've been here ever since."

"Hmm. Reminds me of the good ol' days. They've got a ton of paint on them, but I wouldn't take it off. What do you have in mind to do with them? Do you want to sell them?"

"Do you think they're worth anything?"

"Sure. They're worth something to somebody. You just need to find the right somebody. There are monthly antique periodicals that list items that collectors are looking to purchase. You could list them in something like that. See what happens."

"Sounds like a good idea. How much do you think I should ask for them?"

"I'd just list them for sale. See what you get offered for them. If you're lucky, you might get more than one offer."

"That's what I'm going to do." He turned out the light, and they headed back upstairs.

"I'll be going now. Thank you for inviting me, and thank you for the wonderful dinner."

Paula had her arm around her mother's waist, leaning her head on her shoulder as Franny opened the door to leave. They all said, "Good-bye. Come back again."

Franny headed home to get a good night's rest. She was still a little antsy going into the basement and carefully looked around to make sure all was secure.

9

She watched him as he slowly entered and walked around the front of the store. He stopped and took a closer look at a beautiful walnut washstand. His fingers glided over the top edge to feel the smoothness of the finish. He opened the door and bent down to get a better look at the way it was made on the inside. If she did not know better, she would think that he was interested in the washstand. However, with that medium-priced suit that he was wearing, along with those black oxfords, which were standard issue to all military men and others who worked for the government, she knew he was from the FBI, even if Chief Tenner had not called her that morning to warn her that someone from the agency would be coming to talk with her about the break-in at her home and the store.

"Hello," she called out to him.

When he stood up and turned to face her, she saw a handsome, tall, and slender man with warm brown eyes. A few streaks of gray highlighted his wavy brown hair, neatly trimmed and parted on the side. *A handsome man who is my age*, was her first thought.

"That's a very nice washstand," she said as she walked toward him. "As you can see, it's been well-maintained, and the towel bar is still attached, which is something that's hard to find these days. And that is a decent price for one in such good condition."

"Yes, it is very nice. Maybe a gift for my mother. She loves things that remind her of her childhood years when she lived at her grandmother's house."

"This would make a lovely gift for your mother."

"She does have a few things that were left to her from my grandmother." He seriously pondered over the washstand. "I do think this would probably fit in with what she already has in her house," he spoke in a soft, quiet voice, his brown eyes alive with intelligence.

"I'm sure it would. Nowadays people have more eclectic tastes in their home furnishings. It gives their home a more eclectic and homey atmosphere."

"Yes. I think so too. Well, ah, let me introduce myself." He reached into his inside jacket pocket, pulled out his identification badge, and held it toward her. "My name is Ned Raines, and I'm with the FBI. And if you have a few moments, I would like to discuss with you the matter of the break-in that you experienced. Do you have some time for us to talk right now?"

"Sure. Of course, we can have a seat at my desk in the back. Would you like to have something to drink: coffee, tea, or soda?" she asked as he followed her to her old desk and seated himself on an old handmade, country kitchen chair that was for guests.

"What are you having?" he asked.

"Hot tea. The only coffee I have is instant. Which would you prefer?"

"Hot tea would be okay," he said as Franny went over to an area where they had a refrigerator and a microwave oven. She put a small pitcher of water in the microwave to heat for the tea. Then she heard the bell ring in the back.

"Excuse me for a moment." She looked through the double doors to see who was there.

Davy had heard the bell too, and knowing that Belle was not there to watch the front of the store while Franny waited on customers in the back, he left his work area in the basement to answer the bell. He met the man at the back door and took his receipt. He then walked to Franny's desk to get the original receipt that already had the total charges, including the tax. The original receipt also had an identifying tag number, which was their system of making sure that each piece of furniture was returned to its proper owner.

"Man's picking up those two library tables," said Davy.

He gave Agent Raines a suspicious look as he excused himself to reach around him to reach the box of original work receipts. Davy was showing his man-of-the-house attitude. This was normal for him to act this way whenever a strange man came around who looked like he was something other than a customer, even before the past few days of trouble. He found the work receipt he was looking for, gave Agent Raines another going over with his you'd-better-watch-your-step-here-mister look, and went on to the back to finish with the customer.

Agent Raines waited until after Franny served them both tea and settled down at her desk before speaking, "We had a meeting with the area police chiefs this morning. And Chief Tenner of Martins Ferry brought up the problem that you had at your home a few nights ago. You told him that someone might have entered your house without your permission."

"That's true. There was a light on in the basement when I got home the day before yesterday evening. I didn't know whether to report it or not since nothing seemed to be missing. It was not until the next night after a chest was missing from the store that I thought to check for the extra keys. When I looked for them, they weren't hanging on a hook by the kitchen door, as they should have been."

"I'll need a description of the chest," he said in a slow, thoughtful way.

"Of course." Franny opened a desk drawer, got a sheet of tablet paper, and started writing down a description of the chest. "It is a real antique Chippendale chest, very beautiful." She wrote down the number of drawers and the approximate height and width, as well as the identifying features of a real Chippendale chest.

"You say that as if some of the items in here are not real antiques."

"There are quite a few items in here that are not real antiques. That is why we have the statement "and old furniture" under the name of Johnson's Antiques. Most people do not know the difference; nor do they seem to care. But a real antique piece of furniture has to be at least a hundred years old. Many people think that furniture from the fifties or sixties are antiques. There is a market for all of it at some time or somewhere or another even if they're not antiques.

"We have some dealers, such as Michael Johnson, the owner's son, who primarily deals in real antiques. Then there is Ray Rouse, who deals in real antiques and old furniture. He hauls truckloads of old furniture to New York or Texas. Many people love to decorate their apartments and homes with old furniture. It gives their home a little more character, I guess. So the trick for us here is to try to keep up with the trends and have an excellent display area."

"You certainly do have an impressive display," he said, shaking his head with approval as he looked around the store with his eyes. Then he looked directly at her. "I don't know if you've been watching the television news lately about some recent murders within the tri-state area?"

"Yes. I did see that on the news."

"Well, of course, we're not sure if your break-in has anything at all to do with these other cases. However, for right now, just to be on the safe side, we are looking into every possibility, no matter how remote it might seem to be. So we're going to assume for the present time that maybe there is a possible connection."

"Seriously?" Franny set her tea down onto the desk as she let that information soak into her head.

"Seriously," he said emphatically, looking straight into her eyes.

"What makes you think that?"

"Well, ah. Would I be able to trust you to keep some information to yourself?" he asked, knowing human nature to be what it was that she would most likely tell everyone she knew as soon as he left the store.

However, he wanted to get as much information as he possibly could from her and as quickly as possible. The old FBI ideas of keeping everything secret did not work as well as getting people to understand just what you're looking for and how they might be of help, particularly in this case, where time was of the essence.

"Maybe. If it concerns the store, I should probably inform the owner, Mr. Johnson, of any possible problem. Also I have an assistant, Belle Walker, who's not here today. She had to go to court with her son. Since she is also a partner with me in our share of space here, plus we're best friends, I tell her everything." She knew that he already knew that she would tell those close to her.

"I guess that's understandable. Let me start by saying that we believe that the connection between these murders in the tri-state area is that these people had the habit of collecting old furniture and antiques. That seems to be the one common denominator." He noticed Franny's chin drop a little as the information settled into her mind. "Now your keys to this place have been stolen and a valuable chest is missing. Is anything else missing that you are aware of?"

"No," she said. "I would like to mention that myself, as well as Michael Johnson, the owner of the chest, would not want it known to anyone else that something that belongs to him is missing from the store. He has a very sensitive ego." She smiled. "Seriously, I suppose the primary reason is that it would not be good for our business if that sort of information got out to the public. People might become fearful of leaving their valuable antiques here for repair or refinishing. A large part of our revenue comes from that type of work."

"I understand. That information will be kept confidential. Tell me about the circumstances regarding the missing chest."

"We found it missing the next morning after my house was burglarized." The more she talked, the more a queasy feeling was settling in her stomach as the full enormity of the information about the murders overcame her mind. "It…ah." She thought for another moment. Then her mouth opened, and her eyes grew larger. "You're telling me that you think a murderer was in my home? And, ah, that means that the murderer was in here also?"

"Yes. Quite possibly," he said while looking intently at her, studying her face while she processed what he had said to her.

"Phew! It's awesome to think that a murderer was in my home!" She stood up and paced back and forth. "It must be someone who knows me, somebody I know, don't you think?"

Just then, Davy returned with the office copy of the receipt and a check the man had given for the two library tables. "The man is happy with his tables and said that he'll be bringing in some more stuff sometime next week." Davy could tell by the look on Franny's face that something was up, but he couldn't think of anything more to say so he could hang around them any longer. So he slowly went back to work downstairs.

After Davy had left them, Agent Raines shook his head slowly. "Yes. I think that probably it is someone you know. We would like any help that you may give us in finding whoever is doing these murders."

"What kind of help did you have in mind?"

"I don't know for sure," he said as he took a sip of his tea. "You are one of the few places in the area that restore antiques and old furniture. You have quite a large showroom display of antique furniture." He glanced toward the front of the store. "You meet a lot of other people who are interested in this type of business."

"Uh-huh," said Franny as she mulled all of this information over in her mind.

The more she thought, the more outrageous it was to her that someone she had been in contact with was possibly the murderer. It could even be one of her repeat customers, maybe even someone that she considered a friend. Anything was possible.

"Well," she said as she took another sip of tea.

After a few moments, when she did not say anything else, he prompted her by asking, "Is there anyone in particular whom you would think might be a suspect?"

"No. Not really."

"One thing that we are trying to do right now is to get pictures of some of the furniture that was either in the homes of the victims and is now missing. Also, pictures of furniture that was sold to the victims just before their death. We are hoping to have these pictures within the next day or so. And when we do, would you look at these pictures to see if you recognize any of them?"

"Yes. Of course, I'll check them for you. However, please understand that we get a lot of the same types of furniture in here. I am not sure if this will be of any help to you."

"Well, we'll give it a try. That is all we can do, right?"

"I guess so," Franny said.

"So hopefully I'll return tomorrow with at least some of the pictures. By the way, how do I go about contacting Michael Johnson about his chest that is missing?"

"I'll give you his cell phone number. That's the main way to contact him."

He wrote down the number that she gave him. "I would also like to have a word with your partner. What is her name again?"

"Her name is Belle Walker. She's been taking a few hours off to be with her grandmother who is ill. She had to get her a new medication for pain. I'll give you her address and phone number."

He wrote down the information that she gave him. When he finished writing, she motioned him to follow her as they went down to Davy's work area in the basement. She introduced the agent to Davy and then left them alone, returning to the store area.

A short while later, Agent Raines came back through the store area to where Franny was waiting on a customer who had just purchased one of the picture frames that Belle had restored.

He waited until after the customer left the store. "Thank you for your assistance. I'll be leaving now. Hopefully I'll have some pictures for you to look at by tomorrow afternoon."

"Fine. I'll see you tomorrow then," said Franny as she walked him to the front door.

"It'd be a good idea for you to keep that information about the pictures to yourself for right now."

"Sure. I'll do that," replied Franny.

As they reached the door, Agent Raines stopped and smiled down at her. "I was serious about the washstand. I'll bring the money for that when I come back tomorrow."

"Great. I'll see you then."

"Who was that?" asked Michael with Davy right behind him at the back of the store area.

"Are you two hooked up to radar or something?"

Michael gave her one of his you're-crazy looks. Davy just looked sheepishly at her as he pretended to adjust a latch on a nearby chest. She knew that Davy had told Michael that the man who just left was an FBI agent.

"So he's from the FBI?" Michael asked as he got a cold drink from the refrigerator.

"Yes. You should have let me know that you were here. He wants to talk to you. I gave him your cell phone number."

Michael just gave a long, deep burp after taking a big drink of soda.

"He asked me all sorts of questions about the chest," said Davy.

"What did you tell him?" asked Michael.

"Nothing for me to say to him, except it was here one day and gone the next. He kept asking me if anyone suspicious had been around that day. I told him that everyone who comes here is suspicious for one reason or another." Davy came here from a small town in South Carolina. To him, anyone who paid a lot of money to have old furniture restored that he thought belonged in the city dump was crazy in the head and therefore suspicious.

Franny just rolled her eyes and went about dusting some furniture.

"So what is an FBI agent doing asking questions around here?" Michael asked as he looked directly at Franny.

Franny decided to tell them everything, especially since Michael was the owner's son and he would find out from his father. "Chief

Tenner sent him here because of the break-in at my house. They are checking into the possibilities that there may be a connection to these break-ins and the murders that have been happening in the tri-state area recently. Since this is a tri-state problem, the FBI has been called in to work with the local authorities. According to Agent Raines, the one connection to these people is that they buy antiques at auctions.

"Jesus!" Davy said as he jumped back as if someone had struck him.

"So they think it might be someone connected here some way?" Michael asked.

"Yes, they do."

"So what are they going to do about it?" asked Michael.

"He's looking for photographs of furniture that has been sold to these people at the auction or furniture they had in their home that is now missing. However, do not tell anyone that I told you about the pictures. It really would not be wise to let anyone know about that kind of information. After all, I don't want anyone coming after me."

"I don't see how they will find anything out by looking at pictures," said Michael. "There are too many pieces that look alike. Besides that, you know how it is. Dealers buy stuff at auction. Then it keeps getting sold from one dealer to another until someone gives it a home. None of it with any paperwork."

"It is a far-fetched idea, but they're just looking at any possibilities for information. I certainly hope they catch the no-good SOB soon. The whole idea gives me the willies."

"If you even think that you might have a problem up here, just ring the buzzer for downstairs, and I'll come flying up here. You can count on that!"

"Thank you, Davy. I know I can always count on you. I am so glad that we changed the locks here and Simon changed the code on my garage door. My dog is a good watchdog when I am home. I can hear her barking. So I feel safe there. It is just here with all kinds of people coming through the door. Who knows what some of these people have in mind?"

"You're just going to have to be more careful. You have a habit of getting too friendly with people," said Michael.

"It's what I like about my job, and it's good for business. That's one reason people like coming in here."

Just then, the front door opened, and two women came in to look around. It was more museum visitors.

"Right," Michael said facetiously as he turned around and left through the back way.

"I think it would be a good idea if I moved my workspace up here until all of this blows over. I can make a space just inside the back area. That way, I can see what's going on in the front or the back of the building," said Davy.

"That's a good idea, Davy. I will feel a lot better with you up here. We will just have to spend more time keeping the area clean from all of the sanding before putting on the coat of finish. We can let Kevin and Joey do all of the furniture stripping in the basement."

Davy left to go downstairs to get his worktable and tools to set them up at his new workplace in the back. An older couple came in the front door, pulling an old teacart that they wanted to be refinished. Of course, the telephone rang at the same time. Someone else was interested in getting some furniture refinished.

Thankfully, Belle arrived to help with the customers; however, it was painful for Franny to see that she appeared completely worn out and depressed from the number of burdens in her life that she had no control over. Her son had been sentenced to be incarcerated in a boys' correctional institution for eighteen months. When they had a moment alone, Franny explained to Belle all of the information that Agent Raines had told her about the murders.

"Oh my God! I can't believe this!" Belle exclaimed. "Here I am feeling sorry for myself, and people are getting murdered. And they think it's someone who comes here? Who do you think it is?"

"I can't imagine that anyone I know is a murderer. We'll need to be more alert when people are here. Thankfully, we have Davy to help look out for us." Franny explained Davy moving his workspace up from the basement.

"That does make me feel better. I just can't believe this is happening," Belle said, emphasizing the words with her hands. "I know that God never gives us more than we can bear, but I don't know. I think that I'm reaching my limit."

10

The mountaintops were showing above a cloudy early morning fog that was lingering over the river, giving the valley an exotic atmosphere. Michael was on his way to do a home inspection for one of the local real estate companies. His home inspection business kept the cash flowing, especially during the winter months when the antique business slowed.

Making a left turn onto Fourteenth Street from Main Street, he then drove slowly, searching the even-numbered side of the street. The homes on this street dated back to the 1800s. Most had been neglected for several years and were in a shabby state of repair. Some had been restored to their original beauty and stature. The yuppies had found a place to put their money and a project to restore their enthusiasm for life.

Finding the address he was looking for, he pulled up in front of the house and parked his van. He got out of his van, dressed in a pair of coveralls over his Dockers and shirt. He opened the side door on the van, got out a pair of old work shoes, and put them on. He went up the three steps to the small porch of the empty house. He walked over to the twelve-foot-tall wooden door, unlocked it, and went inside.

Empty beverage cans and food wrappers were lying around on the floors. Apparently someone had been camping out there recently. The old and faded wallpaper was peeled off in places. The house was filthy inside with smells of spoiled food and cigarettes and other odors that he tried not to identify.

He could see that, beneath the dirt and filth, there was beautiful woodwork all around the rooms. Large mantels in the living room and dining room could be made beautiful again when restored. The spiral stairway to the upper floor still had all of the spindles in place. The steps creaked under his weight as he went up to the second floor. The three large bedrooms still had their mantels in place. He opened a hallway door and found the stairway to the attic.

Once up in the attic, a smile lit up his face. *It's a lucky day today,* he thought to himself. Two large walnut armoires in the far corner of the attic were probably made during the same time as the house. These armoires would have been used to store the winter or summer clothing during the offseason. *It's a shame that Allen decided not to come with me today,* Michael thought to himself. *I could have shown him a lot.*

He immediately walked over to inspect them. The armoires had lived a sheltered life, all alone up here in the attic, and both were in excellent condition. Well, he would be taking them both with him.

To inspect the roof, he opened a window and climbed out onto the roof to do that part of the inspection while he was in the attic. Once he finished inspecting that area and the chimneys, he decided to take the armoires down to his van before doing the rest of his inspection. Most people didn't think to take these armoires with them when they moved, primarily because they didn't know how to get them out of the attic. They didn't know that these old armoires were designed to come apart in pieces.

He used a rubber hammer and pry bar that he carried in his coveralls to carefully take them apart without damaging the wood. He neatly stacked the wooden pieces. He would have to make three or four trips to get it all down to his van. Usually, when people looked at an old house, even the realtors were afraid of what they might see in the attic, so if they looked there at all, it was just a quick look. "Oh yes, there's an attic" kind of thing. Most likely, the armoires would never be missed, and Michael would probably get at least twenty-five hundred dollars for each of them when he sold them.

He completed his inspection of the house, checking the wiring, the plumbing, and the foundation of the house. He neatly and carefully filled out the inspection form that he would drop off at the realtor's office. When finished, he went out to his van to take off his coveralls and change into his street shoes. He had a couple of other houses to inspect for a different realty company, but they both had people still living in them. He would do them after his lunch date with Agent Raines. He stopped by the realty company to turn in his inspection forms for the first house and get paid for his work.

"Hello, Rosie," Michael said as he entered Warden's Realty, one of several realty companies that hired Michael to do home and building inspections for them.

"Hi, Michael. How are you today?" Rosie asked as she accepted the inspection forms that Michael handed her. She pulled out the company checkbook and proceeded to write him a check.

"Just fine," said Michael as he sat down and waited for her to finish writing the check. "Is Ben here?"

"No, he's out showing a house," Rose said as she handed him the check.

"Thank you," said Michael. "Tell him I said hello. See you next time."

He headed for the Sesame restaurant in Wheeling for lunch and a meeting with Agent Raines, who arrived shortly after Michael. The restaurant was the size and shape of an old railroad car. When he saw a man walk in and look around the room, Michael nodded for him to have a seat.

After introducing themselves and shaking hands, Agent Raines discreetly showed Michael his identification. Don, the one and only waiter, cashier, busboy, and manager, quickly took their order and ran it back to the only other employee of the restaurant, the cook.

"I guess you are new to the area?" Michael asked.

"Yes, I am. I've been working out of the Charleston, West Virginia, office since I've been with the FBI for the past twenty years. Signed up after four years working with Naval Intelligence. Coming here is a nice change for me. It's a beautiful area."

"It's okay, I guess."

While waiting for their order, Agent Raines wrote down all of the particulars regarding the missing Chippendale chest. After the food had arrived, they stopped talking long enough to eat a few bites.

"This food is delicious!" Agent Raines exclaimed as Don quietly and efficiently cleaned the table next to them and acknowledged the compliment.

After they had finished eating, Agent Raines asked Michael, "Do you suspect anyone of taking the chest?"

"No. Not really."

"The reason that I'm speaking to you today instead of your local police is because the tri-state area seems to have a problem of accidents or murders of people connected to the antique business, either customers or some dealers themselves. You seem to get around the area quite a bit. Have you seen or heard anything that you feel might be suspicious?"

Michael thought for a moment before saying, "No. Can't think of anything."

Agent Raines said, "Well, thanks, Michael for the information and for sharing lunch with me."

They shook hands and parted. Agent Raines went back to the local FBI office located in the Federal Building, and Michael headed for his next scheduled home inspection.

Michael finished his home inspections work for the day and took his newly acquired armoires to Johnson's to be cleaned and restored. After parking behind Johnson's, he put on his coveralls again and unloaded one of the armoires. As he walked into the back area, he saw that Davy had moved his worktable up from the basement.

"What's going on?" asked Michael.

"I'll be working up here from now on. That FBI agent thinks that someone who comes in here might be doing those murders. Franny decided it would be safer if the three of us stayed up here where we can see each other. We'll have Kevin and Joey do most of the paint stripping downstairs."

"Humph," said Michael, not sure if he were going to like this arrangement. He remembered them talking about this for safety reasons, but he didn't think Franny was serious about it.

"Oh. Well, I have this one and another armoire that I picked up. All they need is washing down with varnish stripper and hosed down to clean them up."

"I guess that I'll just go downstairs and do it myself."

"Sure thing," Davy said lightly.

However, in his heart, he felt guilty for not going and letting Franny know that Michael was going to be using store materials for his personal use. Michael was always putting him between a rock and a hard place. Davy knew that one day Old Man Johnson was going to kick off and maybe leave the business to Michael. The best thing for Davy was to stay on Michael's good side.

"Have you found out anything about your missing chest?" Davy asked as he followed Michael to the elevator.

"No. Not yet, but I have a couple people on the lookout for it. When I find it, whoever took it is going to be one sorry person. I can tell you that," he said as he sat the armoire pieces inside the elevator and then walked back to his van to get the rest of the armoire pieces. Davy followed him and helped him to load them onto the elevator.

"Thanks." Michael took the elevator down, unloaded them himself, and took a pail of varnish stripper from the drum marked "store" instead of the drum marked "Michael," just as Davy knew he would.

When he finished working in the basement, he left his armoires to dry for twenty-four hours in the drying room. Upon returning upstairs to where Davy was working, he started pulling off his coveralls. "I'm getting a truckload ready for a trip south within the next couple weeks. So I've got a few other pieces that I want to bring in, that is, if you're interested. I'll pay you to strip and refinish them for me. You could work on them here in the evenings. It'd give you a chance to make some extra money."

"Well, I'd like to. Lord knows I could use the extra money. But I don't know." They'd been down this road before, and he had almost lost his job. "Franny doesn't like for me to work for you here in the evenings. She complains that I'm too tired the next day to do a good job, and she says we use up too much of the store's refinishing materials."

Michael started strutting around in a circle as he talked, "Believe me, she charges me for the materials she thinks I use, whether I do or not. Don't worry about Franny. She can act so high and mighty sometimes. She gets on my nerves. I'm going to be the owner here before too long. Franny will be working for me!"

"Yea. Franny said that Mr. Johnson didn't look like he was getting any better and probably worse. Emphysema is sure a hard way to go. I know that, but still I keep on smoking like an idiot. I keep saying that I'm gonna quit, but I never do."

"So what do you think?"

"Yes, I'll do that work for you until Franny complains. I can't afford to lose my job."

"Okay. How about coming back after supper and I'll have things here for you to start working on?"

"Yeah. Okay."

"Good." Michael started up toward the front of the building, stopped, and turned around long enough to say, "Don't say anything to Franny unless she happens to see you working on it. It's none of her business."

Davy just shook his head. He hated doing anything behind Franny's back. He decided to talk to Franny later that day. He'd tell her that he wouldn't work as late this time as he did before when he did some work for Michael.

When he entered the front part of the store, Michael could see that Belle and Franny were both waiting on customers. He got a bottle of water from the refrigerator, sat down at Franny's desk, and made some business calls.

Other customers came into the store. Michael could see that they would be busy for a while, so when he finished making his calls, he got up to leave. Not soon enough, though, Jerry came in the front door.

"M-Michael. I-I-I was look looking for you," he stuttered.

"Oh yeah?"

"I-I g-got me an old, an old p-pine ca-chest th-that I've been w-working on. Y-you'd like it. I know. I know. It-It's old. Won't cha st-stop by and ta-take a look at it?"

"Maybe I'll stop by tomorrow and take a look at it. If you're sure, it's old." That meant if it were a real antique.

Just then, Franny left her customer to ponder over a decision she was trying to make and walked back to her desk. "I've got a check for you, Michael," she said, knowing that he would have noticed that one of his pieces had been sold. "Some people bought your corner cupboard this morning. They said they could use another one if we get one in."

"I might know where there is one. I'll check it out tonight." He accepted the check she handed him and said, "See you tomorrow."

On his way home, Michael stopped by the cafeteria and picked up takeout food for his own and his parents' supper. When he arrived at their home that was once a small farmhouse located on the outskirts of town, he entered through the kitchen door. He set the food down on the kitchen table and then went into the living room. Most of the furniture in the house was, of course, beautiful antiques, except for the more modern and comfortable living room furniture. There were colorful and attractive antique lamps here and there, along with unique little knickknacks and vases for decoration.

As he entered the living room, he found his father looking like half of the size of the man he used to be hooked up to his oxygen tank, sleeping in his favorite recliner. His mother's gray head was nodding. She also seemed much smaller now than what she used to be with the thin and frail look of an aged woman. She was scarcely awake on the couch, watching her television stories as usual. She hadn't heard him come in, even though he tried to be as noisy as he could, trying to wake them. He had to say her name before she became aware of him.

She jumped up as quickly as she could, not wanting him to think that she had been sleeping. "Oh. Hello, Michael."

"Hello. Hope you like what I brought you for supper today. I have baked chicken with mashed potatoes, green beans, and cherry pie for your dessert."

"We'll love it. We appreciate you going out of your way like you do to look after us," said Sara as she limped due to the pain from her sciatica over to where her husband was sleeping.

Michael went on back into the kitchen to set out their supper for them. He also looked through the cupboards to see what else they might need from the store. He did all of their shopping for them now.

"Richard. Richard," she softly called to her husband to wake him. When he opened his eyes, she said, "Michael's here with supper."

"Hey, Mike. How's it going?" his father asked as he struggled to make his way into the kitchen.

The doctor had made it clear to them that it was important for him to get up and move around as much as possible. They were both happy to see Michael. But no matter what he did for them, their faces never lit up the way it did when Richard Jr. came home, usually one weekend each month from Pittsburgh, just a forty-five-minute drive away.

When he'd finished eating, Michael sat with them and had a cup of coffee while his parents slowly finished their meal.

"Franny came over after you left yesterday evening. She brought us a copy of the monthly financial statements. She and her crew are doing an excellent job at the store," he spoke in a soft voice, often halting to catch his breath. "They work hard, and people like them. And most of all, people trust them to be fair with them."

Michael held his tongue. He had learned years ago that it wouldn't do any good for him to say anything unkind about Franny to his parents, who loved Franny. The Johnsons had never paid much into Social Security during their earning years, so now they didn't receive the full Social Security benefits, which was not much for anyone to have to depend on for their livelihood. They had put all of their savings into the building that housed their store to get it started. They thought they would be able to build the store into a very profitable business that they would be able to work into their old age.

However, it didn't work out quite like that. Soon after they put everything they had into buying the building and getting the store set up, the country went into a recession that lasted nearly two years. They went deep into debt. The only way they were able to survive at all was through the rental of the two apartment units above the store and the profits from the store.

The added stress of trying to survive and hang onto their business increased the speed of the downward spiral of Richard Johnson's health, as well as his wife's despair of life in general. The years of smoking and drinking before they became born-again Christians had caught up with them. Emphysema had settled into Richard's body for the duration of his life. The day that Franny had answered a newspaper ad for the manager of the store a little over three years ago was the day they could finally relax, putting aside their worries of ending their lives in a welfare situation.

It was a struggle at first, especially the difficulties that Franny had in getting Michael to see the proper way to run a business for profit for the store. Her bookkeeping methods were out in the open, on paper. It wasn't the way of many dealers, including Richard and Michael, whose methods were secrets they kept in their heads. She won many an argument with Michael when she could prove her point with her records of the truth. Of course, Richard had to side with Franny, much to Michael's chagrin. Richard and Sara had learned to depend on Franny for all of their financial needs, especially now that they had so many medical expenses.

"Richard Jr. called earlier today," said Sara. "He wants to bring a friend of his home for the weekend. I forget what he said his friend's name is, but they'll be here Friday evening. He said his friend is very interested in antiques, and Richard Jr. wants to show him the store while they're here. Richard Jr. always has the nicest friends."

"Yes, he does. Well, that'll be nice," he said while jealously thinking, *The favorite son is coming home. Isn't that just wonderful?*

"I'm sure Franny and Belle won't mind showing them around the store," said Richard as a knot twisted in Michael's stomach.

Michael loved his brother as well as resented him for having everything that Michael wished for himself, love and respect from his parents being number one. Richard Jr. had confidence and self-esteem. He lived an easygoing lifestyle as a general manager of a large hotel in downtown Pittsburgh, while Michael was filled with insecurity and self-doubt. His life was in constant turmoil as he struggled to find the finest antiques at a good price and find a buyer for them at an even better price. And now Richard Jr. was interested in the store and how it was run. Michael had wondered for quite some time now when that shoe was going to drop, and now it had.

He sat there looking at his parents as they drank their coffee, thinking to himself that it had probably never crossed their minds that Richard Jr. was gay. Michael hoped that the friend who Junior was bringing this weekend would not be too outlandish or weird. Although he had to admit that Junior's tastes in men were usually on the conservative side, the odd one did sometimes show up among the group of them. Hopefully Junior would want to keep his life, whatever it was, in Pittsburgh.

"We'll need extra food for them, if you don't mind, Michael," Sara said as she went over in her mind what meals she might be expected to prepare for them.

"Junior will want to show him around the area, so they'll probably want to go the local restaurants for their meals," Michael said as he realized the struggle that was going through her mind. "I'll just pick up stuff for sandwiches and snacks, a couple of bottles of wine that I know Junior likes, and some soda. If we need anything else, you can just give me a call on my cell phone."

"Okay. We'll just play it by ear and see how it goes." Sara was relieved that not much would be expected of her in the way of meal preparations. She just wasn't up to cooking a large meal for the family, especially with a stranger there to please.

"Well," said Michael, getting up from his chair and cleaning up after himself, "the cleaning service will be here tomorrow, so the house will look nice for your company. I'm going home now. If you need anything, give me a call."

"Good-bye, Michael," they said as he closed the door and left them to get back to their television programs.

He drove the short distance up the road to the double-wide mobile home the Johnson family had lived in while restoring the old farmhouse they lived in now. When Michael married Lila, they moved into the double-wide and made it their home with the idea that they would build a new home of their own on the property. That never happened, which was one reason Lila took the children and went home to her parents.

He had met his wife Lila at a bar in Wheeling. They were both heavy drinkers, the perfect couple to invite for a successful beer party. The two of them were a perfect match, enjoying Michael's sports car and their party life until Lila became pregnant with Natalie. Michael and Lila married because they loved each other and both wanted to provide a safe home for their unborn child. They were both going to quit drinking and straighten up their lives. Lila quit drinking, but not Michael. He felt he'd lost his best friend when Lila wouldn't go out with him to the bars. Lila loved him and tried to help him as they struggled for several years to save their marriage.

The birth of two more children, Carrie, who was now seven years old, and their son, whom they called RJ, added to the stress of the situation. They named him Richard Junior after Richard Jr. because they both loved Richard Jr. and they knew he'd probably never have children of his own. Richard Jr. was proud and thrilled with the child named after him. Although they had never divorced, Lila took the children and moved in with her parents until Michael got his life straightened out.

Another major blow to Michael happened when his father gave the management of the antique store to Franny, sending Michael into a steeper dive into alcoholic despair. He would not have minded Franny managing the store, allowing him to keep his freedom with him as her boss. However, it didn't work out like that. Franny reported only to his father, who usually agreed with everything she did.

He continued his lifestyle of working hard during the day and drinking hard at night. Franny had known several men like Michael while she was in the navy. She was not pushy with him, but when no one else was around, she would softly tell him conventional Buddhist teachings, the same things that were originally the basis for Christianity, which had gotten lost through the years. Somehow he hated to admit that these words and the way they were spoken stuck in his head when nothing else did. Perhaps it was because the Buddhist approached life in such a nonthreatening and logical way.

It was not until this past Christmas Eve in the late afternoon while Michael was driving toward downtown and his favorite bar. As he drove, Franny's words kept repeating in his head, "Take a few moments and sit very still, Michael. Breathe deeply, and exhale slowly. Concentrate on how your body feels, and listen to your mind."

He would tell himself, *The woman is crazy*. But her words wouldn't leave his thoughts. Later at the bar, the bartender was busy, so while waiting for his first beer, with nothing else to do, he did what Franny told him to do. He realized how rotten he felt deep down in his bones. *Christ, these people are so boring*. He noticed how the same people were saying the same things they'd said practically every day that he'd known them, the same boring words over and over again.

After a couple beers, he noticed himself repeating remarks that he had made a thousand times before. Driving home later, seeing the brightly lit houses, he was saddened with the knowledge that people in those homes, including his wife and children, were enjoying love and companionship with all of the warmth of the Christmas season. He knew without a doubt that this was not the way that he was going to spend his life. It was time for him to quit drinking and get his family back together.

With the help of Alcoholics Anonymous, Michael had been free of alcohol for over six months. Lila had started allowing their three children to visit him on the weekends, that is, after he returned from the morning auctions or sales on Saturdays. He enjoyed their visits, and it gave his wife, whom he still loved, a chance for some time for herself. There was a wooded area and a pond for the children's ducks that he had foolishly given them for Easter the previous year. Now he had to worry about their food and shelter during the winter months, so he built a hutch for them with straw for warmth and fed them every day during the winter.

His eldest daughter, Natalie, who was now nine years old, had been begging the past few years for a pony of her own. Lila had agreed to allow her to have a pony for her birthday coming up next month. So now, Michael was having a barn built for the pony. He was making it large enough for three horses, just in case the other children became interested in having their own. If not, he could always use more storage area for his antiques. The construction company he hired had promised to have the barn completed in time for Natalie's birthday.

Lately, he had been thinking that, if all went well, once the barn was finished, he would talk to Lila about building a house out here for the family. However, he wasn't going to rush things. He wanted it to work out right this time.

11

The man drove his van up and out of the valley on a two-lane road that looked as if the road builders had followed a snake while building it many years ago. His eyes were not seeing the beauty of wild and beautiful West Virginia, only the sharp, winding curves of the narrow road ahead of him. His mind was deep in thought of the troubles that had taken over his life.

His wife had taken their children and moved back with her parents, telling them that he had cheated on her. It wasn't his fault if women just naturally came to him with no encouragement from him. The problem started after the children came, and she no longer wanted to go to the auctions and sales with him. That had meant long hours away from home when she didn't know where he was or when he would return home again.

Of course, it didn't help matters for his wife to find out that he had been keeping company with another woman now and then. *Well,* he thought to himself, *I'm a healthy and vigorous man. I need more attention than what she'd been giving me. She's always fussing with the kids and what she thinks they need, not tending to my needs.* He thought that wives understood this sort of thing and overlooked what their men did on the side. He knew dozens of guys who had affairs while they were married. They didn't mean anything by it. Men just naturally did that sort of thing.

But it had been nearly four months now since they'd left. No amount of pleading had changed her mind. She said she felt humiliated with everyone knowing the way that he'd treated her. Besides that, she no longer wanted to spend so much time with just her and the kids at home by themselves. *It's that darn TV set. She's gotten too many high-minded ideas from watching those silly women's programs.*

"Lord, I do miss her and the kids. I'd do anything to get them back," he said out loud as he pulled into the parking lot of a small town bar not far from Wheeling.

And now that bedroom set he'd sold at Rogers Flea Market because he needed food and gas money had turned up at Johnson's. The girl he'd sold it to had said that she was going to strip off the white paint with its colorful hand-painted design herself. But there it was, big as life, sitting there, waiting to be stripped. His only hope was that the FBI man who'd been hanging around Johnson's didn't notice it and find out who sold it to her.

The Barnhart estate auction was going to be too good for him to miss, but after that, he'd load up a rented U-Haul and head for California and spend a few months there until things cooled off. They might be looking for him in Texas, but he wouldn't be there.

He drove into the parking lot of the Hill Bar where his father used to hang out when he was a younger man. Its shabby appearance was a stark contrast to the once-colorful appearance that he'd remembered from when he was a youngster peeking through the door. Three men were sitting at the bar, and only two booths had patrons on a Friday night. When he was here before, people drinking and dancing to a loud jukebox had filled the place. At that time, it seemed that everyone there smoked, and the room was filled with a smoke haze so thick you could hardly breathe. Now the air was fresh and clean in the dimly lit bar. He never smoked himself, so this was just fine with him. He sat down, leaving an empty seat between himself and another man seated at the bar.

"Hey," the other man said in a low voice, acknowledging the arrival of the newcomer.

"Hey," he replied.

"What can I get for you?" asked the bartender.

"Bud Light draft would be good."

"Sure thing." The bartender immediately drew his draft beer and sat it down on the bar in front of him. "Don't think I've seen you in here before."

"It's been several years since I've been here with some other high-school friends," he lied.

His father had come home to get his gun in a high state of drunken anxiety. That was the night his father shot and killed his mother here in this very room. He didn't want to remind anyone of that horrible night that was probably the worst night of his life. All the yelling and screaming and then the loud noise of the gunshot. His father dropped to his knees and cradled her in his arms until the police dragged him away. Now his father was spending the rest of his life in jail. No more alcohol for him.

"Yeah, we thought we were hot stuff coming in here underage. Looks a lot different now, smaller than I've remembered."

"Things have changed a lot in the past few years. We lost a lot of customers when the state passed a law against smoking in public places. If people can't have a cigarette while they're having a beer here, they'll stay home where they can do what they want."

"I'm sorry your business has been hurt by that law, but in my father's case, he used to be a real tough guy type. No one was going to tell him he should stop smoking. Now after several strokes caused by smoking, he can't even wipe his butt and drags oxygen around with him everywhere he goes."

"It isn't just that," the man sitting next to him joined in the conversation. "All up and down the Ohio Valley, steel plants have been shut down. Even the aluminum plant is closed down. Now there's a big push to close down the coal mines. People are moving out of this area like crazy. Our stupid government is trying to give jobs to everyone in the world except workers in this country. They go into politics poor and end up multimillionaires. Doesn't take much to guess how that happens. Foreign governments pay them off to vote on trade agreements that benefit the foreign countries by giving them the factory jobs that helped make our country strong."

"Yeah," said the bartender, "they won't allow the Alaskan pipeline to be built. That would mean a lot of jobs. They remind me of the Africans who sold their own people into slavery."

"Then they gave billions of dollars to so-called clean air companies," he chimed in to be part of the conversation. "Most all of them went bankrupt in no time. The technology is just not there yet."

"I don't know what's going to happen to save this country," said the bartender. "More and more people on welfare. The first thing you know, we'll be like Venezuela. People are rioting in the streets for food."

"They talk about saving the world from global warming," said the man on the other barstool. "They can't save this country, let alone the world."

"I just know it's embarrassing to have such a stupid, greedy government," said the bartender.

He stood up to leave. "It's been nice, guys. Take care."

"Come back again," said the bartender.

He left the bar, drove another twenty miles, and parked near enough to a particular house so he could have a good view of the front of the house and garage. It was now eleven in the evening. He waited a half hour after all the lights were out in the house. Then he opened the garage door, using his latest electronic gadget he used earlier in the day when he followed the homeowner home from an estate sale.

When the homeowner, Wilbur Harris, pushed his remote to open the garage, the code was recorded on his new gadget. He pushed play, and the garage door opened. He waited another half hour to make sure that the noise didn't disturb anyone in the house.

He quietly backed his van up to the garage. As he was loading the dining room set, someone jumped him, striking him in the back of his head. He quickly pulled out his gun that had a silencer and shot the man, killing him instantly. He quickly finished loading the furniture, and with the driver side door of the van open, he pushed the van down to the end of the driveway before he started the engine. He pushed the button on the recorder to close the garage as he drove away. He drove straight to his storage space and unloaded the dining room set before going to the trailer he rented.

It had been getting more and more difficult to work the business the way his father had taught him when he was just a young boy. "Other people are just stepping-stones for you to get what you want in life."

Well, he was well trained on just how to do that, and he was good at it too. The problem was that people didn't let strangers in their door as easily as they did years ago. But now he had found his way around that little problem. It was just bad luck that the man was still awake and heard the garage door open and decided to handle things himself. *He should've just called the police. It was his fault he got shot.*

Now after four months of junk food and sleepless nights, it was getting more and more difficult for him to control himself when stressful situations arose. His usual demeanor was that of an easygoing and pleasant man. But the stress of it all was starting to show around the edges. People tended to understand once they knew that his wife and children had left him.

When he wasn't planning his next strategy, the same tormenting thoughts kept repeating in his head, saying his wife Nora's name a thousand times a day over and over in his head, along with the words, "Nora, Nora, Nora, I'll show you that I can be successful and open my own antique store. Things will be different. You'll see. I waited so long to have my own loving family. I'll do anything to get my family back!"

He said the words out loud. No matter what he was doing, those words kept running through his head. "Work the plan. Use other people as my stepping-stones. Let no one stand in my way! I'll get my family back and soon. Didn't I have a master of thievery teach me?"

The next morning, after a good night's rest, he returned to the storage unit. It was the end unit that faced the hills and away from the road and prying eyes. Luckily no one else was around. He opened the door and then backed the van halfway inside, blocking the doorway. This allowed him the ventilation he needed to work in the storage unit. Also no one could walk in on him as he worked on refinishing some of the pieces that he had been collecting. He had to squeeze himself around the furniture to get to the back doors and open from the inside to get into the unit.

After jumping down from the back of the van, he put on his coveralls to protect his clothes. Then he walked over to his collection and began the work of cleaning and polishing his latest acquisition. Once finished with that, he started working on a pie safe that he had already stripped of its paint. He had thoughts of Nora and the kids playing over and over in his mind. The other pieces, still there, only had old varnish on them. Those, he could just clean and recondition with Brie wax. He'd have all of this finished by the time the load he left at Johnson's would be ready to be picked up.

He would have to rent a large U-Haul van to take the whole load to auction. Now that he had all top-quality antiques, it would be worth the expense and much safer all the way around if he traveled all of the way across the country. He knew that none of the other dealers in the area would go to the auction houses as far away as California. He just needed to do it a few more times to get his business set up real good. Then there'd be no major business worries for life. He'd be able to afford to bid on the better quality pieces, which meant higher profits. He'd be able to set up a place like Johnson's in some other place where he could live a normal life with his family. He'd seen how Franny ran things. He could do the same somewhere else. A better life for himself and his family, that was the plan.

He went to bed that night and enjoyed a restful sleep. He woke up the next morning, feeling refreshed. The murder last evening hadn't bothered him in the least. In his mind, he thought, *A man's got to do what a man's got to do.*

Shortly after Agent Raines arrived at work that morning, he received a phone call from the Wheeling chief of police, Al Tompkins. "We've got another one in the Forrest Hills area. A woman, Carolyn Harris, found her husband dead on the floor of their garage this morning. He was shot once in the head. If the bullet didn't kill him, the loss of blood did. They were at an auction in Pittsburgh yesterday and bought an antique dining room set. As you can guess, that's gone."

"Did she hear anything last night? Any kind of noise?"

"She says she didn't hear anything."

"He must have a silencer on his gun."

"It looks that way," replied Chief Tompkins.

"Jackson and I should be able to meet you there in about fifteen minutes," said Agent Raines.

"Where are we going?" Jackson had overheard the last part of the conversation.

Both grabbed their suit jackets from the back of their chairs and headed for the door. Jackson was an African American who still had his healthy, athletic look about him. He was tall with a more muscular build in comparison to Ned, who was shorter and more slender. Jackson went running regularly and participated in marathon races when he could. He was married with two sons who were also athletic and participated in sports.

"Forrest Hills. Do you know where that area is?"

"Yes, I do. I'll drive."

"We've got another poor soul who bought a bedroom set at an auction in Pittsburgh yesterday. Today he's dead, and the dining room set is gone. I'm hoping for a miracle that it isn't true. My boss isn't going to be pleased to hear of another murder and we don't have a clue of who it is."

Ned's boss had faith in Ned's ability to solve these crimes and capture the murderer. He'd known Ned since he was twenty-three years old and started as a newbie with the FBI. Ned's workspace when he began working at the Charleston, West Virginia, district office was a table with one drawer for pencils and a yellow-lined tablet in a room that he shared with several other agents. There were no windows. A few years later, he was promoted to having an old, beat-up, wooden desk with three drawers on each side and center drawer. With his last promotion, he was given a small office with one window and a much higher quality desk than he'd had before. This was his reward for being such an excellent employee for the past twenty years.

When they arrived at the crime scene, they smelled the scent of death, even though the death occurred in the garage, as they entered the home of the now-deceased Wilbur Harris.

Wilbur's wife Carolyn was distraught. Through her tears, she told them all she knew about the previous evening. "I didn't hear anything after I went to bed last night. I was exhausted after spending the day in Pittsburgh at an auction. I didn't even know that he had not gone to bed. He was watching television in the den when I went to bed. When I got up this morning, I couldn't find him in the house, so I looked in the garage and found him lying on the floor of the garage. I called nine one one, and the police arrived about five minutes later. And now the furniture we bought yesterday is gone. I've got a picture of it on my iPhone."

She handed the iPhone to Chief Tompkins. He sent a copy to his email and gave the iPhone to Ned, who sent a copy to Jackson and himself. The wonders of technology.

"Did he have any enemies that you know of," inquired Jackson. "Maybe someone at work or a relative? Perhaps a former friend who might be holding a grudge?"

"No," she replied.

"Is there someone we can call to come and be with you today?"

"No, thank you. My son and his wife should be here in about twenty minutes."

"Good," said Jackson. "The police officers will be here for a few hours looking for any clues of whoever did this awful thing to you and your family." He gave her his business card. "Call me if you remember anything that might be useful in capturing the person who killed your husband."

Chief Tompkins walked with Ned and Jackson out to their car. He was an imposing figure, especially when he was wearing his uniform, his holster, and gun on one side and nightstick on the other side, along with the bulk of his body.

"You were right in calling us," said Ned. "This is another case of the auction killer at work. It looks like that, for some reason, the garage door was open. The killer must have one of those new electronic machines that record garage-door codes. Let us know if your men turn up anything."

"It's a shame," said Jackson. "I don't know what I'd do if I woke up one morning and found my wife dead."

"That would be a shock. We gotta get this guy quick as we can. When we get back to the office, let's do a background check on Wilbur, and check the people he worked with, friends, and neighbors, just to make sure we cover all the bases. Chief Tompkin's men should have that information in a few hours. Before we do that, let's go by Johnson's and see if anyone brought in a dining room set this morning that looks like this picture."

"Right," said Jackson with a big grin. "I think you're getting sweet on Franny."

"Maybe. Maybe," he said with a grin. "To be truthful, I find her to be a very intriguing kind of person."

"Yeah, I know. The first thing you know, she'll have you walking down the aisle," he said as he started his car and headed toward Johnson's.

When they got to the store, Jackson waited in the car while Agent Raines went to the door. A note stuck to the door said, "Will return in ten minutes." The agent walked back to the car.

"Nobody home. The note said they'd be back in ten minutes. We've got work to do back at the office, so let's head back there."

12

"Belle! Belle!" called Franny.

"I'll be right there," Belle called back from the front of the store, hurrying as fast as she could. Franny's voice sounded distressed. When she got back to where Franny was, she found her bent over, holding her head in pain and perspiring profusely. "My God! What's the matter with you?" She screamed as she bent down to see her better, trying to determine what had happened to her.

"Oh, Lord! I must have fallen and hit my head," she said, holding the back of her head as she tried to get up. The pain was excruciating. "Would you please drive me to the hospital?"

"You don't want me to call an ambulance?"

"No. You take me, please. Oh! My side hurts, and my head hurts something awful. I must have hit the corner of the table when I fell."

"How on earth did you do this? Maybe you should stay still and let me call nine one one. You could be hurt really bad," Belle asked as she helped Franny to her feet. "Davy! Davy, come quickly! Franny's been hurt!"

"Davy's not here. He went to deliver an order. And please, no ambulance. Just put the 'Be back soon' sign on the door. It won't take you long to drop me off at the hospital."

"I don't want just to drop you off at the hospital!" Belle anxiously hurried toward the front door to lock it and put up the sign.

Belle helped her into Belle's old car, praying they would get to the hospital safely. "We have that designer coming at four thirty. That could turn into some nice commissions for us. You have to be here to meet her," Franny stated while Belle snapped her seat belt for her.

Once they got underway, Belle asked her again, "So what happened?"

"I don't know. I dropped a screw cover. It rolled under the table. I bent down to get it, and I must've hit my head when I went to stand up. Or maybe, I don't know, my side is hurting me more than my head. Maybe I have kidney stones again. That caused me to faint or something, and then I hit my head. I don't know. I guess they'll figure that out at the hospital."

Whether it was to block out the pain or she just wasn't right in the head, Belle didn't know which, but Franny talked continuously in a rambling sort of way all the way to the hospital. It seemed so important to her to share her last experience at the hospital emergency room with Belle.

"The last time I went to the emergency room, I had been packing my suitcase, preparing to go to Washington, DC for the weekend. I started feeling some god-awful pains from my kidney area. I've had kidney stones before. It felt like it was the same thing again, so I went to a small local hospital. Only two doctors were there in the emergency room. They both looked as if they were college freshmen, just hanging out in the emergency room. Of course, they had no idea what to do for me. So I just said, 'Look, I've got plans for this weekend. How about some antibiotics and some pain pills to get me through the weekend? I'll come back on Monday.' That was okay with them. They gave me the pills, and off I went to Washington, DC for the weekend. I should mention that they did send me to x-ray. Lord only knows what the result of that was, so I just kept myself filled with pills and had a good time."

"So what was so important that you had to go that weekend instead of putting it off until you felt better?"

"It was the weekend of the dedication of the memorial for women who have served in the military. It's near the entrance to Arlington National Cemetery. I'm so glad that I didn't have to miss it. It was awesome to see thousands of women turn out to support the memorial. Women from all of the military services were there, some from as far back as World War II, up through the Korean, Vietnam, and Gulf Wars. It was great to see them all. Most of the older ones were still in great condition. The younger ones, many of them were in uniform, looked so strong and competent, full of pride. Brigadier General Wilma Vaught presided over the very impressive ceremonies. I can't describe my feelings when the final ceremony ended with several military planes and helicopters flying over the crowd and the memorial. All of the pilots and copilots were women. It was awesome!"

"Well, here we are," said Belle. "Are you sure that you're going to be all right? You're talking kinda weird, like you're in a dream or something."

"I know. Everything seems so surreal. Thanks for the ride and for listening to me ramble on like that all the way here. One of my sisters compares me to Higgins on *Magnum PI*. She swears that I even look like him. Oh! I almost forgot. Would you please call Simon and ask him to take care of my animals for me?"

"Sure, don't worry about them. And if for some reason he won't be able to, I'll take care of them."

"Here's a key to the front door of my house. Thank you, Belle. Good luck with your meeting with the designer. I'll call you later after I see the doctor," she said as she got out of the door and walked into the emergency room registration area.

Belle just shook her head, not knowing what to think, and drove back to the store. She was glad that she could at least be of some help there.

The hospital staff took in Franny right away. Franny surrendered herself to hospital care by taking off her clothes and putting on one of the thin, skimpy hospital gowns the nurse had given her to wear. X-rays were taken, and since she possibly lost consciousness, she was admitted and placed in a room with two beds. *Thankfully*, she thought, *the other bed is empty.* She called Belle at her home since it was now early evening to let her know that they were keeping her there overnight for observation.

"How are you feeling?" Belle asked. Real concern sounded in her voice. "I called the hospital earlier, and they told me that you had been admitted and are listed in good condition."

"I'll be fine after a good rest here," she assured Belle. "How did the meeting go with the designer?"

"Great. She is very pleased with the quality and variety of items we have on display. She is going to try to bring a couple of her customers to the store within the next day or so. We should get a good deal of business from her."

"I'm so thankful that you and Davy were there, Belle. I appreciate knowing that I can count on both of you."

"I'm glad I can be helpful to you, especially now. Davy got back from his delivery and was upset that he wasn't here to help you. We're both going to come over and see you after dinner. I wanted to come home first to make sure that everything is okay here before I came to see you."

"Oh, please don't bother. I'll be asleep in a few minutes. They just gave me something for pain and something to put me to sleep. Would you believe the nurse wouldn't leave until I finished off a glass of water with the pills?"

"I believe it." She laughed. "They're big believers in the power of water. The x-rays showed that I don't have a concussion or kidney stones. So that's good. They're just keeping me here overnight for observation. Plenty of rest is the prescription for right now. Did you get in touch with Simon?"

"Yes. He said for you not to worry. He'll look after your animals for you until you get home."

"Thank you for taking care of that for me. That's a relief to know that they are taken care of. Well, I'll let you go so you can finish getting dinner ready. I'll call you tomorrow and let you know when I'll be getting out of here."

They hung up, and Franny settled in for a good night's rest.

The next morning, she felt sore but well rested. She vaguely remembered seeing Simon and later Belle, who had come to visit her. She was just finishing eating her breakfast when her doctor stopped in to see her.

"Good morning, Franny. What on earth happened to you? Let me take a look at your injuries," Dr. Flynn said as she pulled the curtain around her bed. Franny sat up on the side of the bed so that Dr. Flynn could see her injuries.

When she finished carefully checking her over, Dr. Flynn looked her straight in the eyes. "Your injuries are more consistent with someone having hit you with something rather than a fall. That's what the emergency room doctor suggested, and from the looks of your condition, I agree with him."

"Well," said Franny as she wondered why she would say such a thing, "I would know if I had been in a fight with someone, don't you think?"

"You don't think it's possible that someone could have hit you from behind?"

"It's possible, I guess, just not very likely."

"You can probably plan on going home tomorrow. I'd like to get a few more x-rays just to be sure. We're mostly concerned about some of the swelling you have. Hopefully most of that will go down today. Take it easy, and I'll see you in the morning." She opened the curtain and left the room just as quickly as she had come in.

Shortly after the doctor left the room, a nurse's aide came with a wheelchair and took her to have more x-rays. When Franny got back to the room, she saw a woman in her late seventies sitting up in the other bed. The woman had white hair with long, white legs sticking out from her flimsy gown.

Franny spoke to her as the aide wheeled Franny past her bed. "Hello. My name is Franny." She got out of the wheelchair, and the aide left the room with it.

"Hello," she said in a very pleasant manner. "I'm Geraldine Williams."

"What are you in here for, Geraldine?" Franny got back into bed because it was more comfortable than one of the chairs and she would be at the same level to talk to Geraldine.

"Oh," she said with a long sigh. "My heart's been fluttering or something. I don't know what it's doing. I've been in the emergency room all night while they ran all sorts of tests. I just feel a little worn out now after all of that mess last night. What about you?"

"I fell and hit my head and my side yesterday. I'm feeling a lot better today."

"That's good. You want something to eat?" Geraldine reached into a drawer of the nightstand. She pulled out a plastic bag that was full of bananas, apples, and grapes. And she said as she pulled out a midsized trash bag, "Come and take a look. I've got all kinds of candy in here."

Franny went over and looked inside the bag. A variety of individually wrapped candies filled the bag. There were light and dark caramels, Tootsie Rolls, Mary Janes, and blackjacks. Also there were those white caramels with those dried fruit things, favorites of candy lovers everywhere.

"Umm. You do have all kinds," said Franny as she picked out a few pieces of candy and accepted a banana that Geraldine handed her. "What'd you do, have the ambulance stop at the grocery store for you on the way here?"

"No." She laughed. "My daughter followed us in from the house. She knows how I am about having my goodies, so she stopped at the grocery store and picked up all of this stuff for me. She went home to get some sleep after they got me settled in here this morning. I feel bad because she's going to miss a day of work on account of being with me all night. I know she can't afford to miss a day's pay."

"Well," said Franny, "you know we all seem to make it through these rough pay days, one way or another. I'm sure she felt that being with you when you needed her was the most important thing for her. Are you supposed to be eating this kind of stuff?"

"No. Let me know if you see the nurse before I do."

Franny had just finished eating the banana when Michael walked into the room, carrying a little bouquet of flowers. "Well, what a pleasant surprise!"

"How are you doing?" He placed the flowers on the table. "Belle told me you were here when I went to the store this morning. She and Davy came by last night, but you were sleeping. She wanted to stop by this morning before work, but she didn't have time after tending to her grandmother."

"Yes, I know. She's sure got her hands full taking care of her grandmother and those three awful kids of hers. But I'm doing okay. Just waiting for time to heal. That's about all I can do for now." She looked over at Geraldine and saw she was finally getting some sleep.

"Well, I've got to be going," said Michael in a soft voice, so as not to disturb Geraldine. "I just wanted to stop by and see how you're doing. I know this cannot be much fun for you, so I do hope that you will get well and get back to work soon. I haven't told my dad about you yet. I didn't want to until I saw you for myself. That building and the store are all my folks have as a way of income. They depend on you to support them through their old age."

"They've always been decent to me, and they pay me well enough. Also allowing Belle and me to sell our things from there has been very profitable for both of us. So we've got no reason ever to want to leave. I'll be out of here and back to work in a few days. Belle is very capable of running the place without me."

"Yes, that's true all right. She caught me getting some walnut stain out of the supply room yesterday afternoon. She told me in a very firm way that she was writing that down!" He laughed. "I've decided that my life will be a lot easier if I surrender to your rules. I'm sure that you know just how much I hate to admit it, but I can see now that my dad made the right choice when he made you the manager."

"Thank you, Michael. It's so good to hear you say those words to me. We have been through a lot of stuff. That's for sure."

"Yeah, I know. I just feel that it's time for me to make some changes in my life."

"I've watched you change from an arrogant, self-centered man, just throwing your money away on fast cars, boats, and motorcycles, to a more focused businessman."

"Only because I was forced into making more money to support two households. Lila and the kids in our old place and setting up my place."

"There's not many who could develop a home inspection business and a profitable antique business in just three years' time. Of course, sometimes I do wonder about your methods."

Michael just grinned at her. "Business is business. You've got to do everything you can to stay a winner. I've got to be going. I'll tell Belle that I saw you and you're doing okay. See you out at the store."

"Take care, Michael. Thanks for coming and bringing the flowers. They're beautiful." The nurse's aide came into the room, waking up Geraldine to get her blood pressure and other vital signs. There was no rest for the ill.

Later that evening, Geraldine's daughter visited her and included Franny in their visit as if they'd been friends for years. Belle came by and joined in the conversations, enjoying a chance to relax for a change, sharing in Geraldine's forbidden cache of sweets.

After the visitors had left, Franny drifted off to sleep for the night. She awoke with a start. Someone had been standing next to her bed and was now rushing out of the door. She looked over at Geraldine, who was starting to sit up in bed. "Was that the nurse?" asked Franny.

"No. It wasn't. It was a man! I've been lying here, trying to go to sleep, when I felt someone come into the room. When I saw that it was a man, I sat up to get a better look at him. That's when he took off running out of the room. Do you know who it might've been? It's strange the way he ran out like that, as if I scared him."

"Yes. That was strange." Franny picked up the phone and called Chief Tenner, waking him up at his home, and told him what had just happened and what the doctor had told Franny of her suspicions about the accident.

"I'll send a man over right away to take a statement. I'll also call the nurses' station so they can be on the lookout for anyone who shouldn't be there. I'm going to hang up now. Maybe we can catch him in the parking lot." The phone went dead.

Stan came to the hospital himself to get her statement as to what happened. He had not bothered to comb his hair or wash his face, and he was showing a day's growth of beard. "We didn't find anyone. So tell me again about what happened to you."

"I guess I hit my head on a table and knocked myself out. I don't remember what happened. When I came to, I was laying on the floor. I felt like I had been hit in the head by a two-by-four, and I had tremendous pain in my side. The doctor did mention that she thought it possible that someone had hit me from behind. Now though, I'm starting to feel a little silly. Maybe I've become paranoid and I'm overreacting about seeing a man come into the room. After all, it could be that someone was just in the wrong room."

Stan just shook his head, muttering to himself, "That is a possibility. Well, whoever he is, he's probably gone for the night. One of the nurses did see someone walk past their station. But that's when he was leaving, and he moved too quickly for her to get a good look at him. We don't have the manpower to post anyone outside your door. My guys will try to drive by about every fifteen minutes, to try to keep a watch over the place. What is the name of your doctor?"

Franny gave him her doctor's name, which he wrote down on a note pad that he carried with him.

"That's about all I can do for right now. Take care, Franny, and try to get some sleep," he said, walking toward the door.

After he left, Franny looked over at Geraldine. "Get some sleep after all of this?"

"Does somebody want to hurt you?" Geraldine pulled out the bag of fruit and offered some to Franny.

"I have no idea why they'd waste their time on me."

A short while later, the nurse came into their room to reassure them that they would keep an eye on the room. "It was probably just someone looking for someone in the wrong room. Try to get some rest."

It was late the next morning before Franny was given permission to go home to rest for a couple days before returning to work. She had promised Belle that she would call her so that Belle could take her home. However, not wanting to take Belle away from work, she took a cab home. Sunny Sunday greeted her like a long-lost friend who she thought she might never see again. The cats were equally happy to see her come home but chose not to be so demonstrative with their feelings.

She settled herself in and then called Belle to let her know she was home. Afterward she fixed herself a sandwich and a cup of tea and made herself comfortable in a wicker chair on the front porch, happy to breathe in the fresh air of freedom from the hospital. She had finished eating her sandwich and was enjoying her tea when she saw a dark green sedan park across the street. Agent Raines was coming for a visit.

She could see that he was trying to make out her house number on her outside light pole that had the house number affixed to it. She went to the front of the porch and called down to him. He looked up, relieved to see it was the right house before climbing the several steps that led up to her front porch. She quieted Sunday who had started to bark at the approaching stranger, assuring her that it was okay to let him come up the stairs. Sunday gave her approval of him as he petted her as they walked from the top of the steps to the porch.

"Nice view," he said, trying to catch his breath as he looked out over the town of Martins Ferry, the Ohio River, and the city of Wheeling in the background. "How are you feeling?"

"Much better now that I'm home. Come and have a seat," she said, pointing to one of the wicker chairs. "Would you like something to drink?" She rattled off a short list of refreshments that she had available. He selected a glass of fresh spring water. She left him on the porch with Sunday while she went to get the water.

When she returned with the water, he said, "I went to the store to pick up the washstand, and Belle told me what had happened to you."

"You just never know when something out of the ordinary is going to upset your life. I know I'm lucky that it was not something more serious."

"That's right. You are very lucky. I guess there's some question as to whether or not it was an accident or someone might've deliberately hit you."

"It's so hard to believe that someone would deliberately hurt someone. This place seems like fairy-tale land after living out in the world for so many years. The reality is that you can never really hide from evil."

"Desperate people do desperate things, no matter where they live. When I took the washstand to my office so I could keep it there until my next trip to my mother's house, I had a message from Chief Tenner. When I returned his call, he told me that someone had been in your hospital room."

"Yes. It seems somewhat silly now. It's possible that someone could have been in the wrong room, and my roommate Geraldine scared him as much as he scared us."

"Since we don't know for sure, it's best to take a few precautions until this thing has been resolved. Chief Tenner has assured me that your home is on their list of areas to patrol at least on an hourly base. And you will have to be more aware of what's going on around you. You know. Be more careful. That's about all that we can do for now." He reached into an inside jacket pocket and retrieved several photographs. "I do have some photographs for you to look at to see if perhaps any of these have been in through Johnson's."

Franny took them and started looking through them, not expecting to be of help to him. "These are nice pieces, but I've seen dozens of them over the years. I wish I could be of more help to you, but there's nothing here that sticks out in any unique way that I could say that it specifically was brought in by a particular person. Sometimes people will bring in just one or two pieces at a time. Therefore, you don't bother putting it together in your mind as one or two pieces of a set."

"Well, I certainly appreciate you looking at them. I hope to have more pictures within the next day or so. Maybe something will show up then."

She could tell he was disappointed that she was not able to offer some clue to help him solve the murders that were plaguing the area. "I was just thinking that, judging from the quality of the furniture in those pictures, I think there is a good chance that whoever you are looking for will probably be at the Barnhart auction that is coming up soon."

"I saw that advertised."

"Everyone in the area and a lot of out-of-towners who are in the antique business or want to purchase for themselves are sure to be there. There will be mostly real antiques auctioned off there instead of just old furniture. Similar to the kinds of pieces that are in those pictures."

"It sounds like a good idea for us to be out there. Are you planning to be there?"

"I wouldn't miss it for anything after the way everyone comes into the store talking about it. I want to be able to put in my two cents' worth of appreciation or criticism of the sale." She laughed.

They sat quietly for a few moments enjoying the view. "So what made you want to work for the FBI?" she asked. "It seems like a dangerous profession."

"When I was a kid, I watched all the television programs that featured the FBI men and women as heroes. I grew up thinking that's the kind of man I wanted to be."

"Is it everything that you thought it would be?"

"Yes, I think so. Can't imagine doing any other type of job."

"But it's such a dangerous job. I'll bet that your family wishes you had a different job."

"I've never married. Never found the right one yet, I guess. And my parents gave up a long time ago trying to talk me into a different career field."

Well, that's good news, she thought to herself.

"So have you done a lot of traveling while working for the government?"

"Would you believe that I've never been assigned out of the state of West Virginia?"

"I thought you worked like the military and got transferred every few years."

"No. It doesn't work like that for us. We can request a transfer if we want, but they've found that agents are more effective working in areas they're familiar with, know all the back roads, and so forth. They know where everyone hangs out."

"Seems like a good idea."

"So I'm glad you're feeling better." He stood up to leave. Sunday, who had been lying at his feet, stood up with him.

"What is this? You're going to leave with him too?" she asked Sunday. "I've only been home for a short while, and already you're a traitor." Sunday looked up at her sheepishly. "It's okay. I know how you love to make new friends." She petted Sunday on the head as they walked Agent Raines to the porch steps.

"When are you planning on going back to work?"

"I'll probably go over for a couple hours tomorrow. Give Belle a break for lunch."

"Well, take it easy. I'll stop by when I get some more pictures." He gave Sunday one last pat on the head and went down the steps to his car.

She watched him pull away. He intrigued her. He seemed like a man of mystery to her, the kind of man who had seen more of life than what he wanted to but was so dedicated to his job that he kept going through the dirt for the betterment of society, a worthwhile kind of man who one did not often get lucky enough to meet.

A short while later, she heard Simon pull into his driveway. He looked over, saw her on the porch, and waved to her. "Good to see you home!" he called to her as he walked over for a visit.

"It's good to be home," she said as he climbed the steps to her porch. Sunday was happy to see that she had another visitor. "Thank you so much for taking care of my animals for me."

"Anytime. It was not a problem at all. So how are you feeling?"

"Good. Very good."

"Do you need anything from the store, the pharmacy, or anything? I have to go and get some things anyway, so I thought I'd come by here first and see if you needed anything. I'm making spaghetti for dinner tonight."

"That sounds good. No, I can't think of anything I might need. Thanks for asking."

"You're welcome. I gotta run. I will bring some spaghetti over for you when it is ready. See you later."

Later that evening, true to his word, Simon brought over spaghetti for the both of them, including garlic bread warm from the oven.

"Ohh. This is so delicious! I should have stopped eating a while ago, but I cannot seem to stop. It is so good!"

They were eating on the front porch, where they had pulled up their chairs to a wicker table. Franny often ate on the porch during warm weather since, once seated, no one could see them from the street or either side of the house.

"I don't think that I'm going to be able to move. You'll have to roll me over to my house, or maybe I'll just sleep here on the porch tonight."

As they finally finished stuffing themselves, they sat back and groaned. They heard a car pull up in front, and Franny stood up to see who it might be. It was Belle, and behind her was Davy driving Franny's Mustang. He used the garage-door opener and pulled the car into the garage that was located beneath the porch.

"We thought you might need your car," said Belle.

"Thank you so much, but you didn't have to make a special trip tonight. I could have gotten it in the morning."

Belle just waved her hand, suggesting it was nothing for her and Davy to bring the car home for her.

"I love driving that Mustang. It is so cool!" Davy followed Belle up the front steps.

"Well, look at this, Davy! These two have been stuffing themselves with spaghetti! This looks good!"

"Help yourselves," Simon said as Franny got up to get additional plates and utensils.

Belle and Davy each hugged Franny, telling her they were happy to see her getting well. She thanked them for their help and for bringing her car home. Then she went on to the kitchen.

Returning with the plates and utensils, she said, "You have to have some of this. Simon made it, and it is delicious!"

Davy and Belle dug in and finished off what was left of the spaghetti and Italian bread. In between bites, they told Franny what had been happening at the store. Franny told them about Agent Raines coming by earlier and said he was probably going to the Barnhart auction.

"I hope they catch that person soon," said Belle.

They all echoed her sentiment. Neither she nor Davy planned to go to the auction, although the FBI being there would make it more interesting to them.

"I hate to eat and run," said Davy, looking at Belle, his ride back to the store so he could get his pickup. "But I promised to get some things done this evening."

He did not want to tell Franny that he would be doing work for Michael at the store. He would tell her when she got back to work.

"I have to go too," said Belle. "Thank you for the spaghetti, Simon. You are a great cook! You can invite me to dinner anytime."

They said their good-byes, including Simon, who also wanted to get some work done on his pottery projects. This left Franny to spend a comfortable and quiet evening alone with her family: Sunday and the cats, Harry, Larry, and Rachel.

13

The Center Market and the whole south Wheeling shopping area, including Johnson's, was crowded with out-of-towners who were in for the upcoming sale at Barnhart's. Luckily Franny was feeling strong and healthy now that she was well rested from her injuries to her head and side. She could keep up the pace of dealing with a large number of customers that had been streaming into the store since they opened that morning.

Since this area was noted for its glass, Marge, the glass tenant of Johnson's, anticipating the probability of a good sales day for her glassware, came into work the day with Belle and Franny. The three of them had barely time for the morning coffee before starting to ring up sales.

As usual, Jerry came in to nose around, even with several customers from out of town in the store. He walked around areas that were not his rental space, muttering to himself but still loud enough for customers nearby to hear him.

"J-junk. J-junk. T-this is al-all j-junk!" Then he walked over to his area, running his hand over his table that he had proudly refinished himself. "N-Now th-this is wh-what I-I call nice."

Several people moved away from him and then soon went on out of the front door. Belle looked over at Franny with a look of disgust on her face.

Franny walked over to Jerry and spoke to him in a quiet voice, "Jerry, I need to talk with you in the back right now."

With a bewildered look on his face, he followed her to the back area and on out the back door. Franny wanted to be sure that none of the customers could hear them.

Facing him, Franny said, "Jerry, you just crossed the line. Go and pull your truck around to the back here, and Davy will help you load your furniture. I don't want to see you here ever again."

"Y-Y-You c-c-can't d-do t-t-that!" Jerry said in a loud voice. "T-that kn-knock on y-your h-head m-must have m-m-made y-y-you c-c-crazy!"

In a calm and controlled voice, she said, "I've never liked you being here, and I will not put up with your nonsense any longer."

"Y-you're n-n-not the o-owner h-here. R-Richard J-J-Johnson t-t-told m-me t-that I-I-I c-can s-s-stay h-here f-for as l-long as I-as I w-want t-to."

"I run this place, not Richard Johnson. I've put up with you all this time, out of respect for him. But you're too much for anyone to have to put up with. The sad thing is that you probably thought that you were being cute. Believe me when I say that you were not cute!"

"I-I-I'm g-going t-to c-c-call R-Richard."

"You go ahead and call Richard. You either move your furniture out of here yourself, or I'll have Davy move it to the basement!" Franny turned around and went back into the building, locking the back door behind her.

As she walked toward the front of the store, she thought to herself, *What is it with so many men? No matter how old they get, they still think that everything they do is as cute as when they were three years old.*

Jerry stood there flabbergasted by what had just happened, especially because the only person in this world who he genuinely admired was Franny. To have someone you admire cut you down was especially hurtful.

"Something has gone wrong in her head. She's not thinking right." Then he walked around to the side of the building where his truck was parked and drove home to call Richard.

When Franny arrived back at the sales room area, she had a nice surprise. Richard Jr. was talking with Belle.

"Well, Richard, what a nice surprise!" she said as she accepted his warm hug.

"You're looking great, both of you! Let me introduce my friend, Steve Colter."

Steve had been looking over a beautiful armoire, and at the sound of his name, he immediately came over to warmly meet Franny. He had already been introduced to Belle. He was a tall, handsome, and very pleasant man with fair skin coloring and natural blond hair. He had a well-dressed look just wearing blue jeans and a T-shirt.

"We want to go to the big Barnhart auction tomorrow, which will take up most of the day. Then on Sunday, we want to take the folks, Lila, and the kids out for Sunday dinner. Of course, I wanted to bring Steve here to meet you two and show him around the store. He is very interested in antiques and has quite a few of them in his apartment. I've wanted to show him the area, so the Barnhart auction is a good excuse to come back home for a visit."

"It's great to see you home again. It sounds like it's going to be a busy weekend for you. If you would like to show Steve around the store, just go ahead, and if you need anything, just give a yell."

"Thank you. I appreciate that. We'll try not to bother you though. Things look busy here today."

"A lot of out-of-town people here for the auction," Franny said before going to help Belle wrap a purchase.

Richard took Steve on into the back of the store to show him how the business was set up to operate. He described the sales area and the work area that was right behind the sales area, the loading dock area, and the stripping and refinishing area that was in the basement.

After showing Steve around the store, they stopped by the counter to say good-bye to Belle and Franny.

"We'll be seeing you. We're going across the street for a fish sandwich if you'd like for us to bring something back for you?"

"No, thank you. It was nice to meet you, Steve. I'll probably see you both at the auction tomorrow."

"Oh, that's great! Good-bye, Belle."

She waved good-bye to them from across the room, where she was with a customer.

When they had a quiet moment, Franny told Belle that she had told Jerry to get his stuff out of here and not come in here ever again.

"Hooray! Hooray!" Belle said joyfully.

"I second that," said Marge. "I never could stand that man. I don't know why you put up with him for as long as you did. Although it is sad that his wife passed away."

"I know. Nevertheless, that's no excuse. He has always been a pain in the butt. I should have thrown him out a long time ago. I already feel relieved that he's gone."

Later in the day, while wrapping a couple picture frames, Franny looked up to see Agent Raines standing nearby, hoping to catch her attention. She noticed how his face lit up when she recognized him.

"Sorry to come at such a busy time," he said, looking at her with a sincerely apologetic look on his face. "But I would like to speak to you for just a moment."

"Okay. Wait for me at my desk in the back, and I'll be with you in just a moment." She finished with her customer and quietly told Belle and Marge that she was taking a lunch break. As she walked back toward her desk, Marge and Belle gave each other a knowing grin. "If you don't mind, I need to eat some lunch." She headed for the refrigerator. "I have some sliced chicken roll and a tomato here if you would like a sandwich or something to drink."

"No. Thank you. I've already eaten. However, you go ahead with your lunch. It looks like you're back in the swing of things. How are you feeling?" he asked, trying to make small talk while she quickly prepared her lunch.

While he waited for her, he reached inside his jacket, retrieved a stack of photographs, and set them on her desk.

"I'm feeling fine. Thank you." She sat down at her desk and took a bite of sandwich, and then she picked up the stack of photographs. "I don't know. It's as if I told you before. These things do look familiar. They are things that are popular, so I have seen several of these same types of pieces. I don't think that I will be of much help to you. I wouldn't want to send you on a wild goose chase."

"Well, I know that it's a long shot. But you never know what might cause something to click in someone's head and be of real help to us."

She took a drink of soda and continued looking at the pictures. She took her time at looking at the pictures. She wanted him to know that she was interested in being of some help. Near the bottom of the stack of photos, she saw something that made a light bulb go off in her head.

"This one here." She looked more intently at the photograph to make sure she was not mistaken. "I'm very sure that this furniture was here just last week."

"What makes you think that you've seen that particular one before?" he asked as he leaned over her shoulder to see the picture she was looking at.

"Because it's the only set I've seen with that unique hand painting on it. It doesn't look like that now though. All of the paint has been stripped off, and now it's down to plain wood again without the hand painting on it. It'll look like a hundred other pieces now."

"Do you remember who brought it in for stripping?" he asked, allowing just the slightest hint of anticipation to show in his voice.

"No. Not right offhand," she said, taking another bite of the sandwich before she reached into a side drawer of her desk and pulled out the completed work receipts.

She carefully looked through them, searching for the one she remembered seeing. Since the person was someone she did not know, she would have his or her name, address, and telephone number in the proper place on the form. Not finding the receipt she was looking for among the completed forms, she looked through the work-in-progress forms. She didn't find it there either.

"That's strange," she said, looking perplexed. She carefully looked through all of the receipts once again. "Oh no!" She looked at him in disbelief. "One of the receipts is missing!"

"How can you tell?"

She showed him how all of the completed receipts were filed in numerical order according to the receipt number in the upper right-hand corner of each receipt. The receipt number 0571 was not in the completed file; nor was it in the work-in-progress group.

Agent Raines sat there thoughtfully for a moment before quietly saying, "I think it's safe to say that your injuries were not an accident. Someone got you and Belle out of here long enough for them to take the missing receipt."

"We would have heard if someone came in through the back. Or maybe we heard the bell, but we were busy at the time and thought Davy would take care of whoever was there. However, if he had left to make a delivery, I guess that someone could have come in without our knowing that they were here if we assumed the bell we heard was Davy leaving."

"Once inside, whoever it was could have hidden behind a piece of furniture until just the right moment."

"This is getting to be too much! I guess I should be grateful that I didn't receive worse injuries than what I did," she said as she took another bite of her sandwich.

"That's what makes me think that it is probably someone who knows you and likes you, I might add. Although you were injured, I think they probably did not anticipate that your falling would add significantly to your injuries. Also since they got what they were looking for, I am sure that the word has gotten around that the FBI drops in here on occasion. I don't think that you need to worry about any further break-ins or attacks."

"That's certainly good to hear."

"Can you take a moment to trace back to the day that the receipt might have been written? If we could isolate that day, maybe you will be able to remember something about the person who brought the furniture in to be stripped."

"Okay. I'll try." She looked at the other receipts that were written the same day as the missing receipt. With the help of the receipts, she thought back to that day and the events that happened throughout the day. "Oh, now I remember. The pregnant girl brought that furniture. I remember because I had to help her unload her truck. She was eight months pregnant at the time. I was worried about her lifting so much weight in her condition. She was a farm girl, strong as a horse. I hate to admit it, but she did most of the lifting. Hmm. I can't remember her name or where she lives."

"Please try to think of something that might help you to remember her name."

"I'll try, of course. However, I cannot imagine that this girl would have anything to do with those murders. She must have bought the furniture from someone else, not knowing its history."

"In either case, we need to talk to her as soon as possible. I would also like to have the names, addresses, and telephone numbers of the other tenants here at Johnson's. I've already spoken with Michael Johnson, so I already have his information. I also talked with Belle the other day when I came by for my washstand and found out that you were in the hospital."

"Yes. I have a list right here, but we need to scratch out Jerry Manning's name. This morning I asked him to get his furniture out of here and not come back."

Agent Raines gave her a surprised look but didn't say anything.

"Personality conflict," said Franny. She handed him a list of all of the tenants' information. "Marge Helmond, our glassware tenant, is working with us here today. I'm sure she could stand a break if you'd like to talk with her here?"

"Yes. That will help to speed things up a bit. However, let me ask you something. Of all the people you deal with here, who do you think might be the most likely person who could have done these awful crimes?"

"I don't know," she said, noticing that things had slowed a bit in the front of the store. "It has been driving me crazy, trying to think of all the people who bring work in here. Antique dealers are, by nature, secretive about what they have and where they got it. Sometimes they come in here bragging about what they got without admitting where they got something. They don't want anyone to know where they got something, for fear that someone else checked it out and turned it down as not being worth the price. They are very sensitive about things like that. The men seem to be more sensitive about that than women are. Michael Johnson and Jerry Manning have even had someone else bring something of theirs in for stripping, trying to hide the fact that it belonged to them.

"Another way that the men and women dealers seem to differ is that, when women buy something for their home, they usually keep it in their home for quite a while. With the men, everything is for sale at any time. That's one problem that Michael's wife Lila would get so enraged about. He would show up at the house with someone to show him or her their dining room suite, bedroom furniture, or whatever Michael thinks the person would be interested in buying. Michael would give his sales pitch on the stuff, and the next thing Lila would see was Michael emptying out drawers onto the floor and then her furniture being loaded up into a truck. A few times they would have to sleep on an air mattress until he got some more furniture in there. Everyone else thought it was funny. However, it was not funny to Lila. She threw him out of the house the last time he did that to her."

"That would be rough on a woman."

"But in things like that, there are no serial numbers on furniture. Unless it is a rare or unique piece, you are never going to find it. From the looks of these pictures, you're looking for fine quality antiques. Something like the cabinet that Michael had that is now missing."

"Does Ray Rouse or Jerry Manning deal with antiques of the same quality as those in these pictures?"

"Ray Rouse does for sure. He deals with all types of old furniture and good quality antiques. Jerry Manning likes to give the impression of being a big-time dealer. However he doesn't have the money to deal with this kind of quality." She cleaned up her desk after finishing her lunch. "If you're finished with me, I'll send Marge back to talk with you."

"Yes," he said. "That will be fine. Thank you for letting me intrude on your lunch this way."

"No problem." Franny went up to the front to let Marge know that Agent Raines wanted to speak with her now.

Marge's eyes grew large with terror. In a hushed voice, she asked, "What on earth for! I don't know anything. Why would he want to talk with me?"

"He's very easy to talk to. You don't have to be afraid of him. He'll just ask you a few questions. That's all."

Marge, filled with fear of the unknown, went back to talk with Agent Raines. Franny was soon busy waiting on customers. This was probably the busiest day they had ever had at the store.

"That Barnhart auction is drawing in the people. This whole town is going to benefit from that sale," Belle said.

"Yes. I'm getting excited myself about going out there tomorrow morning."

"That place is too rich for me," said Belle. "I think that's why we're so busy. Some people are afraid that it might be too much for them out there, but they don't want to go home with nothing."

"I think you're right."

Just then, the telephone rang. Belle answered and then held the telephone for Franny. "It's Richard. He wants to talk with you."

"Hello, Richard. How are you today?" She'd been dreading this call. "I'm sorry, Richard, but it feels so good to know that we don't have to put up with him anymore. Another thing is that he makes racial remarks about Belle. We are getting busier and busier with people coming from the Pittsburgh and the Columbus areas. We can't have a crazy man coming in here every day calling everything that we have in here junk and making racial remarks out loud. He'll run people off, just like he did today, and we can't afford to have that happen ever again."

"I understand how you feel. We're pleased with the way you're running things there, and I'll stand by any decisions you make. I'm calling only because I promised Jerry that I would. But please, Franny, keep in mind that he doesn't have any other friends. His sons and their families have disowned him because he is a pain in the butt to everyone. Since his wife died, you've been the only friend who he's had besides me."

"I know all of that, Richard. He does it to himself. He's old enough to know how to behave like a normal human being."

"His family was rough on him when he was a kid. I'd appreciate it if you would please try to figure out some way that he can still sell his antiques from the store."

"I'll think about it," Franny promised him before they hung up. "Uhhh!" She shook her head. "Richard wants me to find a way that Jerry can still sell from the store."

"I do feel sorry for him," said Belle. "Especially since his wife passed away and that girlfriend with those kids left him. It would be okay with me as long as we didn't have to see him every day. If maybe he just came in to refill a space after we sold something."

"I guess we could work something like that out with him if he would stick to it. Well, I am going to let him stew about it for today. I need to make it clear to him that he needs to respect us women. I don't want him to think that he can just call Richard and everything he does is going to be okay."

Just then, Marge and Agent Raines came walking up toward them.

"Thank you, ladies. I know how busy you are today, and I appreciate your helpfulness," he said as he walked past the counter toward the door.

"Come back anytime," said Franny as the three of them said good-bye to him.

"He is such a nice man!" Marge said after Agent Raines closed the door behind him. "But I didn't have anything to tell him. He asked me if I had any suspicions about anyone I know who does business here. I told him that I couldn't imagine anyone I know of who would do such a horrible thing to anyone."

"I don't know if I will ever feel safe again, even after they catch the guy. Look how often it is that one of us has worked here alone. Anyone could have come in here and done something to us. We need to make sure that there is always two of us here during business hours," said Franny.

"I'm glad that Davy is working upstairs now," said Belle. "Especially when you are out doing estimates in people's homes."

"Just don't hesitate to use that buzzer to get Davy up front here, either one of you," said Marge. "Even if you are not sure if there's a danger. It's better to be safe."

A few minutes later, Joanna came in to look around the store to see if anything new had been added since she was last there. She always took her time in looking at everything. Poking into things around the store was a good way for her to prod her memory and feelings of things that happened in her past to give her ideas for her book writing. She had on a beautiful summer dress that was covered with a miniature print of pale pink roses. She was also wearing a white summer hat with white gloves and attractive white heels. Franny suspected that Joanna sometimes dressed like the main character in the book she was currently writing. She believed that, because she knew that Joanna always did her shopping or dinners out at restaurants during the middle of the week when the stores and restaurants were less crowded. Joanna had spent so much time alone with her reclusive lifestyle that, when she got around crowds, she felt overwhelmed with fear of the mass of breathing humanity.

The three of them greeted Joanna with the usual, "If we can help you with anything, just let us know."

Then they let her alone to look around for as long as she pleased without having someone hovering over her and interfering with her thoughts. Since it was getting close to closing time, there were only a couple of other customers in the store while she was there.

"Well," said Marge, "I don't know about you two, but I've had a hard day, and I'm tired. I'm not used to so much activity. I think it's time for me to head home."

"We're glad you were here to help us today," said Franny. "I don't know how we would have managed without you. It is especially nice that you were here to answer all of those questions about the glassware. Belle knows more than I do about glassware, but I keep trying to learn about the different pieces. There is so much history to the different periods that it boggles my mind."

"What I know about glassware you could put in a thimble," said Belle. "You know how often I have to put a customer on the phone so they can ask you a question about something."

"I've heard you answer a lot of questions," said Marge. "You know more than most people, and that's what counts. And I'll see you, girls. Franny, I'll see you at the auction tomorrow. Belle, I'll probably see you both on Monday. We can make sure my inventory is straight, and of course, you can pay me then."

"I'm glad you did well today, Marge. Get a good rest this evening. Because I know that it's going to be a busy day at the auction tomorrow. Good-bye."

Belle echoed good-bye, and Marge left through the back door, where her car was parked behind the store.

"Do you see anything that interests you today, Joanna?" Franny walked over to where Joanna was looking at a couple of old chairs.

"I am looking for a couple chairs for the front porch of the little house at the farm. But I don't know if these will do or not."

"We can hold them for you if you would like to take a few days to decide."

Joanna had spent a small fortune at the store, so Franny was willing to do almost anything to please her. Plus Franny considered Joanna to be the most interesting customer that came into the store.

"That would be nice. If you're sure you don't mind?"

"I don't mind at all. Anything for you, Joanna."

"Thank you. I know it's closing time for you, so I'll call you on Monday and let you know one way or the other. I don't expect you to hold them for me forever." She opened the door to leave. "Good-bye, girls."

Franny picked up the chairs to carry them to the back area. "I just love that woman," said Franny. "I hope I can have her energy when I'm her age."

"Me too," said Belle. "Even though her mind does seem to run in slow gear sometimes, at least it never stops."

Davy came up to the front to say he was ready to leave for the day. "I have everything ready for Kevin and Joey to strip furniture downstairs tomorrow so I'll be able to work up here with Belle. Don't spend too much money at the auction tomorrow."

They normally closed at one o'clock on Saturdays. That gave people who work during the week time to come in and either pick up or deliver their furniture. And for those just shopping, they usually did that in the morning and then had a sandwich at the fish market across the street for lunch.

"I'm not planning to buy anything. I think it will all be out of my league. Especially since Ray Rouse gives us such a good deal on picture and mirror frames, and he seems to have an unlimited supply. I've never been to an auction of this magnitude before. I'm just going for the excitement."

"Well, we'll think of you while we'll be hard at work here. Have a very good time tomorrow. By the way, Franny, I meant to mention to you that Michael has asked me to do some work for him in the evenings." He felt a dark cloud pass over him, but he needed the money. "It would be here with your permission, of course, or at his place. It would be easier for me if I could do it here. I promise I won't stay too late at night and be tired the next day. And I'll be sure to keep track of the materials I use."

Franny thought for a moment before answering, "I'll trust you, Davy. However, at the first sign of things not going right here during the day or you start getting cranky with us so we can't stand to work with you, it'll be over."

"I promise that won't happen this time. I'll just work a couple hours at a time. That way it won't get out of hand like it did before."

"Okay, Davy. See you when I get back on Monday."

"I think we are ready to leave too," said Belle. "See you tomorrow, Davy."

After eating her dinner, Franny went over to Simon's workroom to see if he were still planning to go to the auction with her in the morning. The door was open, so she stepped inside. He was standing there, looking over his finished pottery pieces.

He turned and looked at her with an elated look on his face. "I'm finished! Everything is packed and ready to put into the van for the show in Columbus. I am ready! I'm usually going crazy trying to get everything done right up to the last minute. I finally have my act together. I'm so proud of myself. What a relief!"

"And the good thing is," said Franny, "everything is beautiful! By this time next week, you'll have tons of orders to fill."

"Wouldn't that be nice? I sure hope so. It would be nice if I could do this full time. I'm getting a little burned out on teaching. Oh well, how would we live without our dreams? So are we still on for tomorrow?"

"Of course we are. It's going to be exciting. It's quite an event for this area."

"I have such a feeling of freedom. What do you say we go to The Tavern and have a beer?"

"No, thank you. You go ahead. We had a busy day today at work. I need to get my rest. But I'll see you in the morning."

Besides, she thought to herself, *he is much younger than I am and will probably appreciate a fun night out with his friends.*

"Okay. We can go for breakfast in the morning before we go to the auction."

"Good. See you then."

When Franny arrived back at her house, she noticed the light on the answering machine was blinking, so she pushed the message button. A message from Belle said she wanted Franny to give her a call this evening, no matter how late.

Franny dialed Belle's number and got a busy signal. *It's probably one of her kids on the telephone,* she thought. She tried again a little later; the telephone was still busy. *Lord only knows how long those kids will be on the telephone.* Since Franny wanted to go to bed early, she decided to make the short trip to Belle's house and find out why she wanted to talk to her this evening.

As she approached the house, she could see that all of the lights were on, and several people were on the front porch and inside the house. A feeling of foreboding filled her. She said hello to the people on the porch, and without knocking, she entered the living room. Sadness filled the air, and several people were weeping as Franny walked on through to the kitchen. Belle was there, showing a woman where she kept the tea and coffee. She had been crying, and as Franny hugged her, Belle told her that she felt guilty because she checked on her grandmother when she got home from work and she seemed okay then. So Belle got busy fixing supper for the family. When she took some soup into her grandmother, she found her dead. It was like her grandmother waited for her to come home from work before she would let go and pass on.

"But I should have been with her. Someone should have been with her," she sobbed.

"You were with her. She died peacefully while hearing the comforting sounds of you fixing dinner in the kitchen. What could be better than that?"

Belle seemed to appreciate that way of looking at it. Franny helplessly uttered the usual words of comfort, which always seemed to be inadequate. But what else could one do?

She stayed at Belle's until late in the evening, talking with her and the other mourners. They spoke of what a fine person Mrs. Walker had always been and how she had helped them with their children at various hard times in their lives. Several spoke through their sadness and tears of her words of wisdom that had helped them through the difficulties in their lives as well as how she had been there to help Belle and her children.

The next morning, Franny called Davy and told him about Belle's grandmother. Davy would be on his own as far as management of the store. Of course, he would have Joey and Kevin there to help him if necessary. Franny felt comfortable with Davy being in charge of things there. Before she had hired Belle, it was just her and Davy. He was often left there alone to deal with the customers while she went out to give estimates. Of course in those days, she did most of her estimates either in the early morning hours before the store was due to open or after closing hours. This made for some long and tiring days. The hiring of Belle was a real blessing for Franny and Davy.

Simon called to let her know he had survived his little celebration at The Tavern the previous night.

"Good morning, Simon. I'm glad to hear that. I was wondering if you are still interested in going to the auction this morning. I thought you might want to rest this morning. Belle's grandmother passed away yesterday evening."

"I'm sorry to hear that. I know how close she was to her grand-mother. This is going to be hard for her and the kids."

"Yes. It'll be hard on all of them for quite a while, but it's some-thing we all have to go through someday."

"That's the sad thing about life." He paused for a moment. "I still want to go to the auction with you, that is, if you're still going."

"Yes. I might be as well. Aunts, uncles, cousins, and other friends will be filling Belle's house. If you don't mind, we can stop by the deli and get a plate of food to drop off before we go to the auction."

"Sure. That's a good idea."

"I'll probably stop by again this evening for a short while after the auction. Hopefully she'll be able to get some rest. So I'll see you in about thirty minutes then."

They hung up to finish getting ready for the auction.

14

"Oh. There's Marge over there," said Ann. She jumped up and waved her arms until Marge saw her and worked her way over to the seat they had saved for her.

"You'd better quit waving your arms," said Margaret. "Jed will think you're bidding."

"Phooey, he knows I'm not bidding," she said as she sat down.

They all greeted Marge as she sat down.

The bid on the corner cupboard keeps going up higher and higher until finally, it was just Michael and Ray doing the bidding. It kept going for several more bids before Ray quit bidding. Franny looked over at Ray and saw him looking back at her with a grin on his face. Franny just shook her head, acknowledging that she understood that Ray had deliberately run up the bid on Michael. He knew how Michael could not stand to lose something he had his mind set on getting, especially not wanting to lose to Ray, whom Michael considered his main competitor.

On the other hand, Michael would still make money on the cupboard. Also he wanted to make an impression on the out-of-towners right from the beginning that he was willing to go as high as it took him to get the pieces he wanted. He hoped that this would discourage them from bidding too high on other pieces he had chosen to make a bid on.

The next item was a dining room set consisting of a mahogany Queen Anne-style table with six chairs and a magnificent-looking sideboard. Margaret bid at the beginning then; even Michael dropped out as it rose much higher than what he thought it would bring if he were to take it to the Georgia auction, where he normally did business. Apparently someone other than a dealer had purchased the set for his or her home.

Several other furniture items were sold before they finally got to some of the things from inside the house, including the painting that Franny hoped to take home. Jed started with some miscellaneous boxes. By mixing these types of items in between the large furniture items, it helped to keep the auction more interesting and exciting, especially for those who were only interested in bidding on the less expensive items. Jerry ended up with one of the miscellaneous boxes; somehow he found value in those things.

Then Jed held up the painting for all to see, mentioning that there had been some damage to the painting and frame, and the bidding began. Franny could not believe it when two others started to bid on her painting. The problem was that some of the people there wanted to have something from that house to keep, as long as it did not cost too much. Happily, the bid ended with Franny as the winner. She still considered it a great bargain at fifty-five dollars.

Franny knew that Simon would not want to take a chance on missing the bidding of the vases, but she needed to get up and walk around for a while. The wooden folding chairs were causing her pain in her lower back.

"Oh, I hate these chairs. I need to stretch and take a walk anyway, so I'm going to go and pay for my painting and take it back to the car. Does anyone want anything to eat or drink while I'm up?"

Concentrating on what was coming up next for bid, Simon handed her the keys to the car and waved her off. The others nodded a "no, thank you" on the drinks. Each time they placed an item in place for bid, there were murmurs of oohs and aahs and talking among themselves from the audience. It was a bit of a noisy bunch today, perhaps because they were outdoors.

The bidding on the next item started as she carefully made her way, trying not to step on any toes to the end of their row. As she walked toward the back of the chairs section, a few people who had been repeat customers of Johnson's gave her the nod and a smile, which she pleasantly returned to them.

Michael was standing with Richard Jr. and his friend Steve to the right at the midway section, giving her a jab as she walked by them. "Of all the nice stuff here to bid on, you buy that thing?"

She stopped for a moment, saying, "I like that thing." Then she made a face at him. "You can buy me something nice if you want to."

Richard Jr. and Steve laughed softly and flashed her one of their radiant smiles. Standing to the side of them was Allen, who was smiling at her remark.

"He left that filthy Hoosier cabinet outside your door one morning. I'm sure you remember that one," said Michael.

"Yes, I certainly remember that filthy thing." She smiled. "Where the heck did you get that thing?"

"Someone was cleaning out their barn and had stuff sitting out by the road for sale. It looks good now. You'd be surprised."

"See you guys. I gotta go hide my treasure so someone doesn't steal it from me."

They all laughed as she walked away. Ray was standing near the back of the crowd with some other men. She recognized two of the men, Walter and Leon, who had picked up and delivered furniture to the store for Ray.

"It looks like you found you a fixer-upper," said Ray in a soft voice as he smiled at her.

"Oh yes. Something to do in my spare time at Johnson's," she said brightly, smiling a hello to Walter and Leon.

"I got one on Michael for you because of the way he treats you. I knew he wouldn't let go of that cupboard, no matter how high the bid."

"Thank you. I've had times when that would have made me feel better; however, he and I are finally starting to get along after all this time."

Some of the glassware was being auctioned while they talked; apparently Ray was not interested in bidding on any of those.

"I was talking with Richard Jr. and his friend earlier. It sounds like he will be getting into the antique business," said Ray.

"Oh, is that right? He showed his friend Steve around the store yesterday. I overheard him explaining how we do everything; however, I didn't know that Richard Jr. was interested in actually getting into the business. Of course, we were busy, and I haven't had a chance to talk to him about anything like that. I wonder if Michael is aware of that plan."

"Do you think that he might come back here and maybe take over at Johnson's?"

"No. I think he likes living in Pittsburgh; however, if he does come back, Belle and I could set up our place in one of those areas being restored in the Downtown Renovation Project. So, however it turns out is okay with me, but I don't think that it would be fair to Michael to have Richard Jr. take over the store."

Franny could hear the other paintings being auctioned off at several hundreds of dollars in the background as they talked.

"I can't see the old man giving it to Michael," said Ray, "but it might get interesting around there."

More furniture was carried to the selling area, so Franny wished Ray good luck and walked over to where Millie and Sara were seated. Both were busy as people were still arriving as well as others paying for their purchase items. One of the men took her receipt over to the painting to make sure the registration numbers matched. Since they did, he brought the receipt as well as the painting over to her, congratulating her on her purchase.

"Are you afraid that someone's going to take your painting?" Stan asked, teasing her about being so quick to get her painting after the bid.

"Clowns are everywhere," she responded, looking at him dressed in Levi's jeans, wondering if she looked as good for her age. "No, I know it needs work. However, I am looking forward to working on it in my leisure time. It will be a challenge but fun."

He gave a soft chuckle. "How are you feeling?" His eyes darted around the loading area while he was talking to her.

"Just fine, thank you. I'm back to work, and everything seems to be okay."

"That's great to hear. You're not leaving now, are you?"

"No. Those wooden chairs are killing my back. I just need to walk around a bit, so I'm going to put my painting in the car."

"Oh, I see." Then in a much lower tone, he asked, "Have you remembered anything more that might be helpful in our investigation?"

"I think her first name might be Beth," Franny replied in the same, quiet manner. "I can't remember her last name. I know she lives somewhere on a farm and she has either already or should be having a baby any day now. I wish I could be more helpful, but that's all I know."

"Well," he said, shrugging his shoulders, "if that's all you know then, that's all you can do. I'm sure that something will come up and we'll be able to track her down before too long. We are checking the hospitals and the recent births. At least now we know that we're on the right track. Having a direction to take makes a big difference, thanks to you."

"Thanks." Knowing that Stan wanted to be focused on what was going on in the loading area, she said good-bye, picked up her painting, and walked down the lane toward her car. A few others were walking ahead of her. *Probably other victims of those chairs*, she thought to herself.

Enjoying her nice, leisurely walk down this beautiful country lane made her think for a moment of how nice it was in the country. Maybe she should move to the country. Then reality set in. She would love it in the country until it got dark. Then she would be terrified.

As she neared the area where her car was parked, she became aware of two other women talking to each other, also heading for their car nearby.

"Oh my God! It's pregnant Beth!"

Franny ran over to the woman's car, and not knowing what else to say, she blurted out, "Hey! Don't I know you?"

"Hi," Beth said hesitatingly until she recognized Franny. "Oh sure, how are you?"

"Just fine, thank you. I was just trying to remember your name."

"It's Beth. Beth Koch. I still haven't gotten a finish on that furniture you stripped for me. I decided to wait until after the baby was born, which I think is going to be today. My water broke, so my sister is taking me to the hospital."

"How wonderful! What hospital are you going to?"

"Wheeling Medical Park."

"That's great! Good luck," she said, stepping back from the car as Beth's sister had already started the car and was revving the accelerator, eager to get going.

Oh wow! Franny thought as she quickly ran to her car and put the painting into the trunk. She slammed down the lid and hurried back down the beautiful and peaceful lane. As she neared the loading area, she excitedly motioned Stan to come and talk with her.

"What's going on?" he asked, looking concerned as he hurried toward her.

"I just talked to pregnant Beth! She just left for the hospital with her sister!"

Stan immediately called Agent Raines on his radio and then asked Franny which hospital. She told them, and while they waited for Agent Raines to meet with them, Stan asked her other questions, such as what kind of car they were driving and if Franny got the license number.

"It's a red Oldsmobile. I was too excited to think about getting a license number." Franny was disappointed with herself for not being more alert. Then she remembered, "Her last name is Koch." Saying that made her feel more pleased with herself.

Agent Raines joined them, and Stan filled him in on what Franny had told him. "Good work, Franny. This is wonderful! Thank you," he said with a great deal of sincerity. Then he quickly radioed others in his group. "Stan, you keep on with what you are doing here. We need to be aware of everything that happens here today. I'm just taking one of my men with me to the hospital. I'll call you later with an update."

His man joined him, and they quickly left for the hospital.

"Whew," said Franny as she left Stan to concentrate on his job. She was too excited to return to her seat, so she walked over to where she could stand while watching the auction and contemplated all that had just transpired. Feeling that someone was watching her, she turned around to see Jerry was standing nearby, looking at her.

He sauntered over to her. "I-I don't k-know w-what y-you're so m-mad about."

"Jerry, I don't know what to do. You have alienated even your own family because of your obnoxious behavior." He was looking at her as if he couldn't imagine that anyone would think him obnoxious. "Belle and I are not going to put up with it any longer."

He looked crestfallen. "L-l-look. I-I'm s-s-sorry. C-Can't we w-w-work s-s-something out?"

She could see that he was severely distraught over being thrown out of Johnson's. "Yes, we can, that is, if you stick to the rules. In particular, if you can't say something nice, don't say anything. We can try this for a while. If things don't improve, you're gone. I have several others who want a space there, so I don't need your crap."

"I-I'll c-c-change. Y-y-you'll see. W-we'll g-get a-along j-j-just fine." The relief at solving this problem was written on his face. "T-thank you, Franny. Y-Y-You w-won't be s-sorry." He quickly walked away before she would change her mind.

After standing there a while, she calmed down enough to go back to her seat. She decided to keep the episode of pregnant Beth to herself as well as her meeting with Jerry. They were all happy to see her return to the group.

Franny was glad to see Michael win the bid on the beautiful bookcase secretary, hoping that he'd set it in his space at Johnson's before taking it South. Margaret was overjoyed to get the bedroom set that she had fallen in love with, along with a couple of small tables. Ann was happy to be taking home a beautiful doll to add to her collection.

It was nearly noontime before Simon could bid on the vases. The bid went too high on the one he wanted; however, he was quite content with winning the bid on another one he had looked at earlier. They all shared in his excitement at having made his first purchase at an auction.

More glassware was put up for bid, for which there were quite a large number of competing bids. Marge was pleased to end up with several pieces. Although there were still several furniture pieces left to be auctioned, the five of them decided it was time for them to leave.

"We're just not as young as we used to be," said Marge as they helped to load her glassware into the trunk of her car.

Later that evening, Franny's curiosity about pregnant Beth and her connection to the murders was getting too much for her. So she placed a call to Stan at his home.

"Hi, Franny. I was just going to call you. I gotta tell you that I am worn out after being out there all day. Anyway, I just hung up from a call from Agent Raines. Apparently, the girl bought the furniture from that big flea market at Rogers, Ohio. She feels awful that it was stolen from someone who was murdered. It will eventually be returned to the victim's estate. By the way, she had a baby boy."

"I'm sure she's happy with a boy. So it'll probably be a few days before they can check that out?" Franny was disappointed that he didn't have anything more exciting than that to tell her.

"Investigations are seldom easy and take time. Have a good night."

"Yea. You too." She disappointedly hung up the telephone.

17

The auction was over, and now there was the sadness of Belle's grandmother's funeral. Franny and Davy joined Belle and her family and friends at the cemetery. The weeping women in their thin heels tried to keep their balance on the steep hill as they gathered around Grandmother Walker's casket while the minister committed her to the grave. After which, the woman's sobs crescendo into wails of agony. The women hung on to each other as they staggered back to their cars.

Franny and Davy followed the other mourners to the church basement for food and refreshments. Everyone appeared calm by the time they arrived at the church. Belle would be taking a few days off before returning to work.

Five days had passed since the Barnhart auction, and there was still no news about any breakthrough in the murder cases. As usual, life went on at Johnson's and everywhere else in the world.

The store looked refreshed with a change of storeroom displays. Older displays had been put on trucks for points unknown. Recent purchases from the Barnhart estate and other sales were now beautifully displayed for the next month or so. If not sold, they would be on the next truckload headed out of town.

Margaret's old Victorian bedroom set was prominently displayed in the store now that she was sleeping on a bed that had belonged to one of the wealthy Barnharts. Michael had brought in one of the corner cupboards and a dining room set that he purchased at the auction. He'd left that morning in his furniture truck for the big auction house in Atlanta. The glassware that Marge bought at the auction had made an impressive display, even more so with its vibrant colors. Jerry had been unusually quiet, which seemed weird, when he brought items in and set them up for sale.

As the morning sun shone through the front window of Johnson's, a wholesome and attractive young girl, tall with long, blonde hair loosely pulled back in a bun, was holding a piece of woodwork that was refinished at Johnson's. Belle, as part of her first day back to work, was patiently explaining to the girl who was upset that the woodwork had various shades of color because of the natural grain of the wood.

"But I don't want it like this. I want it all one shade." The girl was now close to tears.

"Then what you want is painted woodwork," Belle said for the third time. "We can paint it for you, if that's what you prefer."

"No. No. I want a natural finish, but I want it all one color." She was emphasizing her words, believing that Belle didn't understand what she meant.

Belle was becoming as exasperated with the girl, as the girl was with her when Joanna, in a colorful flower print dress and sandals, breezed into the store. Observing that Belle was busy with a customer, she walked on back to see if Franny might be available. She found her working on some paperwork at her desk.

"Good morning, Franny."

"Joanna! What a treat! What're you up to this morning?" Laying down her pen, she stood up to greet Joanna.

"Oh, ah." Hesitating, as she always hated to impose on anyone, she replied, "Well, I was wondering if you would do a favor for me."

"Sure, if I can, I would be happy to help you. What is it that you need?"

"I found two old rocking chairs listed in the *Green Tab*. I was wondering, if I decide to buy them, would you pick them up for me and take them out to the little house at the farm?"

"Certainly. Just let me know, and either Davy or myself will pick them up and take them out to the little house for you."

"Wonderful!" A smile brightened her face. "I called the people before I left the house, and they still have the chairs. So I'm going to pick up my sister, and we'll go out there, take a look at the chairs, and make sure they are what I want for there. Thank you so much, Franny. I knew I could count on you. I'll call you later."

"You're welcome. Anytime that we can help you with anything, please just give us a call," she said as she walked with her up to the front of the store. After Joanna had left the store, Franny went to assist Belle in dealing with the dissatisfied customer, repeating what Belle had already told her that, to achieve all one color, it would need to be painted. However, a lot of people loved the natural look of wood and its various shades of color.

The girl decided to go home and think about it.

About an hour later, they received a call from Joanna, saying she did buy the chairs and gave Franny the address, telephone number, and directions to where she could pick them up. It was about lunchtime when Franny decided to go and get the chairs.

"I think I'll get those chairs before those people decide to sell them again to someone else."

"That's probably a good idea," said Belle. "You know that Joanna will be worried until she gets them out to the farm."

"I'll probably be back in about an hour and a half, if that long. I'll just pick up some fast food to eat on the way."

"Yeah. You need to be careful about that eating and driving thing that you do."

"Oh, I'll be careful. See you later."

She was thinking to herself that Belle was starting to sound more and more like her grandmother. It was amazing how that happened to people, or maybe she'd just never noticed that before.

She drove to the nearby small town where Joanna had bought the chairs. It was an old coal town whose better days had been gone a long time now. Locating the address, she parked in front of the house that was just like the neighboring houses, an old shotgun style with a wooden frame built by the coal company for its coal miners back in the days when the company owned the town. Only a few of these houses showed signs of being loved and maintained.

The house she was going to was not one of those. Stepping onto the front porch, she walked gingerly to the front door because the porch appeared to be unsafe and worried she might fall through to the ground below. After knocking on the door, a large, disheveled man in his middle to late thirties opened the door with a suspicious look on his face. He was wearing old, dirty, and baggy sweatpants that were barely hanging on below his large, hairy beer belly. He topped that off with a filthy T-shirt that only partially covered the hideous and obscene girth.

"Yea?"

"I'm here to pick up the chairs for Mrs. McKenzie."

"You from Johnson's?" he asked, opening the door to allow her to enter.

"Yes," she answered.

He motioned her to follow him into the house, which was not something she wanted to do, but she went anyway. The house looked as if they were clearing it out, preparing it for sale. Furniture from all of the rooms was stuffed into one room. All of it was for sale, according to the man. The chairs that Joanna had bought had been set aside in a room on the left. The chairs had layers of white paint on them. Several areas were showing through where the paint was either chipped or worn off, and of course, they were filthy dirty.

The man, with a grunt, picked up one of the chairs. Franny picked up the other one and carried them out to her van. With a brief "thanks," she closed the back door to the van and got away from him as quickly as possible.

The drive through the countryside to the farm was rejuvenating. She had the two front windows down, and the wind blowing through her hair was refreshing and uplifting. The landscape was so full of life with all of its colors and spring newness, with the occasional sighting of wildlife. Two trips to the country within a few days gave her the feeling of having been blessed. Thinking to herself that most people would have thrown those chairs into the dump, they were perfect for the little house that sat at the back part of the farm. Joanna would probably put another coat of paint on them herself, and they would look just fine. Joanna had told her that the little house reminded her of her childhood, and it being part of the property was probably a strong selling point when she bought the farm.

She arrived at the turn-off to the farm, slowed for the sharp turn to the left, and quickly passed through the main gate. A long, dirt road went up the hill to the main house that sat on the knob of the hill with a fantastic view of the countryside for miles around. The main house was completely restored and furnished with beautiful and expensive antique furniture, as though someone lived there. The restoration was a project of love, and the main house could easily pass as one of the homes depicted in *House Beautiful*. However, no one lived on the farm. Joanna and her husband lived in a beautiful Victorian house in town, spending each winter at their home in Miami.

On pleasant days, Joanna loved to come out to the farm alone and work on writing one of her romance novels or spend pleasurable and relaxing time working in the garden. Her husband, a retired businessman, spent nearly every afternoon and evening in a bar near their home in town. A man who had always been appealing to women, even at his age, he flirted with other women and had affairs with several of them through the years.

The single-track dirt driveway was a quarter-mile long, up a steep hill, before it reached the back part of the house where they usually parked. Midway up the drive was another single lane that went left to the little house. That lane curved below the main house, and just before making the left turn onto that lane, she briefly caught a glimpse of the back part of a van that was parked behind the house. A man was seen looking in a side window. *That's odd,* Franny thought to herself. *Joanna didn't mention that someone else would be there today.*

She would call Joanna later, tell her the chairs were delivered, and mention the van so she knew about it. She drove slowly on the dirt track, below the front of the main house and around past an old apple orchard area. Beyond the orchard was a clearing where the little house sat off to the right of the road, out of sight of the main house. The little house looked like a duplicate of the house on the television series *Little House on the Prairie.* It was hard to imagine how a family could live in one of these small houses, especially through the harsh winter months, with no running water or electricity, so far away from other human beings.

Joanna had told her that there were six children in her family, plus her parents. Their home was similar to this one in size and style. Franny felt disheartened as she thought of all the hardships Joanna and her family must have endured through those years of living in such a cramped, little house. The love the family shared with each other was what Joanna remembered.

Franny pulled up to the front porch and parked the van. Getting out of the van, she was even more aware of the peacefulness and the natural beauty of the area. She was just starting to lift the first chair out of the back of the van when she heard another vehicle coming down the track. A van pulled up behind her van and stopped, taking Franny by surprise because the road track ended at this little house.

She quickly set the chair back down in the van to see who was in the other van. It was the same color as the van she saw parked behind the main house. The birds had stopped singing, and an ominous feeling permeated the air around her.

As the door of the van opened she held her breath as she saw the man getting out of it. "Allen, what're you doing here?" She asked in a surprised voice.

"Hi, Franny." He nervously tried to act nonchalantly as he got out of his van. "I told the people who own this land that I'd take a look at some antiques they might want to sell."

"That's strange. Nobody told me that someone else would be coming out here today. Do you know the people who own this place?" Franny was suspicious because Joanna would sell to Michael before she'd sell to anyone else.

"Sure, ah. A guy I met at the bar last night told me to come out here and take a look at some things he wanted to sell. Here, let me help you with those chairs," he said as he took the chair out of her hands and carried it to the porch. "I heard you were in the hospital. How are you feeling?"

"Fine, thank you. We can just leave them on the porch." She reached for the other chair and pulled it closer to the edge of the van, still wondering why Joanna had not mentioned to her that someone else would be coming out to this empty farm today.

It must be that her husband arranged for Allen to come out here without saying anything to her. She watched him as he set the chair on the porch instead of coming back for the other chair. He tried to open the front door.

"I'd kinda like to see the inside of this old house. Do you know where they keep the key?" he asked while looking through the front window.

"No. I've got to get back to the store." As the ominous feelings continued to flow over her, she hurried and set the other chair on the porch.

She did know where a key was hidden. However, she did not intend to tell Allen. He had always been pleasant and treated her with respect; however, for some reason today, she couldn't seem to put aside the uneasy feelings she had about him being out here in this isolated area. *Probably because,* she thought, *I didn't expect him and also because there is no one else for miles around.* She wanted to get away from there as quickly as possible. Just then, she heard another vehicle coming down the track.

Upon hearing the approaching vehicle, Allen became noticeably more nervous and turned to leave. "Yea. I guess I'd better come back another time when they're here. Looks like you've got company. See you later, Franny."

"Are you following me?" she asked, recognizing the driver as Agent Raines. He was on his cell phone as he got out of his car with a suspicious look toward Allen, who had turned his van around and headed back toward the main drive. However, now he is blocked in by Agent Raines's car. He ended his call and asked her if everything were okay by his look without saying the words aloud. Franny just shrugged her shoulders.

"Maybe," he answered, not telling her that he'd been following her since she'd left her home that morning.

He was going to wait outside of the gate to the farm until he saw someone run and jump into the van, following her down the track and out of his view. That was when he'd decided to follow her to make sure she was going to be okay.

"Is this someone you know?" He asked Franny.

"Yes. That's Allen Ryder. He's related to the Johnsons's. Allen is sitting in his van facing them; raised his hand in a half wave as he waited for Agent Raines to move his car to the side so that he can get around him and away from the farm.

Agent Raines phone rang. It just took him a moment to answer then get back into his car and moved it aside for Allen to leave; which he did immediately.

Not pleased that she had been followed, Franny was both annoyed and glad that he was there. However, since he was there, she decided to make use of him. "Would you do me a favor?"

"What did you have in mind?" he asked suspiciously.

"Follow me back up to the main house to make sure that nothing's been tampered with." She felt terrible about saying those words to him because she'd never had any real reason ever to think badly about Allen.

"Sure," he said, getting back into his car. He also wanted to check out the main house.

He followed her back up the track to the main drive, making a left-hand drive up to the back door area of the main house, completing a phone call before parking his car beside hers.

Franny made a phone call to Joanna. "Hey, Joanna. I'm out at the farm and put the chairs on the porch. There was someone out here who wanted to look at some antiques your husband told him about. That's what he said anyway. He's gone now."

Franny could feel the steam coming through the phone. "No. There shouldn't be anyone out there but you. I'm not selling anything! Get that man out of there!"

"A lawman friend of mine is with me to check things out and make sure he has left. I'll call you back in a few minutes."

"The doors and windows are still locked, and it doesn't look as if anyone has been tampering with them." Agent Raines said after they had checked all around the house.

Just by looking through the windows, they could tell that nothing had been disturbed inside of the house.

"I guess I was overly suspicious," said Franny.

"That's understandable with all that's been going on around here. Everyone's going to be jumpy and suspicious until this is all over with and the killer is put in jail."

"I guess so. I hope you find that guy soon." Then suddenly feeling brave, she asked, "By the way, have you had lunch yet?"

"No, I haven't, but I'm going to be busy for a while right now. That van is the one we have been looking for. I called in the license number when I first drove up behind it. I was just notified that reinforcements were waiting for him at the main entrance."

"Allen! Allen is the one who has been doing these murders?" she asked with an incredulous look on her face. "Oh my God! This is so incredible! He's Richard Johnson's son!"

"It's a very good possibility that he is the one responsible for the murders. We'll know more after we arrest him and get his fingerprints to see it they match one we might have found at one of the crime scenes. If it isn't him, we may at least be able to get information from him that would lead us to the killer. That van is the one that was used by the person renting the space at the antique mall where Beth Koch purchased her furniture. So we'll see what happens."

The sheriff's car with Sheriff Tom had Allen stopped at the main entrance to the farm. "You wait here." Agent Raines left her to join them. By the time he reached them, two other police cars blocked Allen's van.

As she watched them, she thought to herself, *This explains why I was not hit hard enough to do any real damage. I had the misfortune to fall at an odd angle and hit something else on the way down. Richard would never forgive Allen if he had seriously hurt me. Then being afraid that he had hurt me, he went to the hospital to check on me for himself. The Johnsons and especially Michael are going to be devastated if the killer turns out to be Allen.*

When they had Allen in one of the police cars, Franny drove toward the main gate to leave the farm. She slowed to a crawl as Agent Raines approached her van.

"So, ah," said Agent Raines, leaning with his hands on the driver's side door, making sure that she was listening to him. "If you're still hungry, we can go and get some lunch. It will take them about an hour to get his personal information and have him fingerprinted and processed."

"No, thanks. I don't feel very hungry right now," she replied. Ordinarily, she would have been overjoyed at the invitation, but with all that had happened, she just wanted to get back to the store. "By the way, why were you following me?"

"Just a hunch. I thought that, since you've been the main connection in this case, you might still be in danger."

"I'm grateful you showed up when you did, although I don't know for sure that I was really in any danger. Do you really think he's the murderer?"

"We found antiques in storage units that he rented. I think we found Michael's Chippendale chest that was stolen. We'll need him to identify it sometime soon."

"Michael's out of town right now. He should be back in a couple days. I guess you'll be going back to Charleston now that your work is pretty much done here."

"No," he said, resting his arm more comfortably and intimately on the van door where the window had been rolled down. Observing her in a very pensive manner, he informed her of his new job assignment. "I've been assigned to head the West Virginia, Northern Panhandle District. My office will be in Wheeling. I was wondering, since you're familiar with the area, maybe you could help me find a nice place to live."

Just a trace of a smile appeared as she looked him in the eyes and answered, "Sure. Just give me a call."

As she drove off, she reminded herself that, with her luck and his good looks, they'd be fifty million women staking out his place twenty-four hours a day. She wouldn't get her hopes up; however, it would be nice to have some fun for a while.

Arriving back at Johnson's, Davy and Belle took a coffee and tea break while she told them everything that happened at Joanna's farm.

"At this time, he is considered the alleged murderer. The cases are still being investigated. Can you believe it? He's probably the one who hit me on the head and stole that receipt! Of all people, Allen!"

"My God! What on earth made him do such a thing?" Belle asked, shocked to hear that it truly was someone known to them who was being accused of those horrible and senseless crimes.

"Money," said Davy. "That and trying to hang onto a woman who doesn't love you is the root of all evil. You mark my words." He pointed his finger to emphasize his words. "When it all comes out, you'll see that a woman is at the root of his problems."

With that, he got up and went back to work to get a project finished before the day's end. He wanted to keep Franny happy so she would have no complaints about him doing work for Michael in the evenings. The truth was that he had always liked Allen and was upset about his arrest. Davy understood how despair can make you do things you would not ordinarily do. Thoughts of Allen would occupy his mind for this afternoon.

After he had left them, Franny and Belle pondered the dilemma they were feeling. They wanted the murders to end and the guilty one arrested; however, the possibility that someone they knew was the alleged murderer was upsetting to them.

Franny took a deep breath and then nosily exhaled. "I just feel so weird about all of this. Joanna will probably never feel safe at the farm again."

"That's sad. She didn't deserve for anything like that to happen on her property. It's a good thing you arrived when you did. That probably prevented Allen from actually breaking into the house," Belle observed.

"Yes, that is one good thing." Then after a moment, Franny asked, "Ready for another shocker?"

"I don't know if I can take anymore, but give it to me anyway."

"After they arrested Allen, Agent Raines invited me out to lunch."

"And you didn't go? I'm disappointed in you. When was the last time that anyone has asked you to go anywhere other than Simon?"

"It has been a long time; however, to be honest, I had asked him first before he got all tied up with the Allen thing. So maybe he was just being polite."

"I don't think so. I've seen how he looks at you, and I think he likes you."

"He's going to be staying on here. He's being assigned to the Wheeling office. So I guess that I'll find out how serious he is. I have no desire, and I'm too old to fight the competition for any man. He also asked me to help him find a place to live. Do you have any suggestions?"

"Not right offhand. This is getting chummy. Things could get interesting around here. To change the subject, my son Eddy is allowed to have visitors this Saturday, so if it's all right with you, I would like the day off so the girls and I can go and visit him."

"That's fine. I'll work on Saturday."

Just then, the telephone rang, ending their break.

"Time to get back to work."

That evening, the story of Allen's arrest headed the local and national evening news.

The next morning, Michael called. "Is it true that they think Allen is the murderer?"

"It looks that way. They think they've found your missing Chippendale."

"Well. That's one good thing," he said soberly. "I'm on my way back. Probably drive straight through."

"Take care."

She no longer hung up the phone before it was ringing again. "Oh. Hello, Agent Raines. Yes, I can call you Ned."

Belle grinned as she made change in the cash drawer.